Wyldblood

Issue 12 - Spring 2023

AF260513

Wyldblood Magazine #12 - Spring 2023

© 2023 Wyldblood Press and contributors.
Print ISBN-978-1-914417-16-0

Publisher: Wyldblood Press, Thicket View, Bakers Lane, Maidenhead SL6 6PX UK.
www.wyldblood.com **Editor:** Mark Bilsborough. **Fiction editor** Sandra Baker. **Subscriptions:** 6 issues epub/mobi/pdf delivered to your inbox £20. 6 issue print subscriptions £35. Single issues available worldwide via Amazon and from wyldblood.com/shop

Submissions: we are regularly open for submissions of flash fiction, short stories and novels – check our website for our current status and requirements. We are a paying market. We also need artwork, people to review us, and people to review *for* us. Email contact@wyldblood.com

Issue 13 will be published in July 2023

Editorial

We're just back from *Eastercon* (the UK's main Science Fiction convention) and it seems lots of people have come back with an unwanted dose of covid, including our unfortunate Fiction Editor, Sandra. It's massively ironic that in an environment where I saw more masks and more active covid policies in place than I have for ages (like a mask only room) that so many people should succumb. I don't think the organisers could have done anything more to keep people safe (there's no current compulsory mask mandate in the UK and seeing people masked in public – even in crowds – has become rare), but it's an uncomfortable reminder that we can't just carry on like we did before. Here's hoping that everyone gets well soon.

Anyhow, *Eastercon* itself was a great success and it's nice to get conventions back after a rocky few years. I thoroughly recommend them – a great place to mingle with writers, artists, publishers, readers and fans and to catch up with old friends (and make new ones). This con was in an overpriced hotel in Birmingham (the one in the rainy West Midlands, not the sunny one in Alabama) but the canny ones do it more cheaply. *Eastercon's* a fairly typical mix of expert panels, workshops, guest author interviews, games, dealer tables, book launches, parties and presentations and they even managed to throw in a trip to a Parkrun this time. Cosplay is (thankfully) optional, but it's nice when people come across all steampunky. Most of these events are run by volunteers and have a good, homely, community feel – Eastercon's a good case in point – well run and inclusive.

There are some great conventions still to come, with *Cymera* (Edinburgh), 2-4 June), *Fantasycon* (Birmingham, 15-17 Sept) *Bristolcon* (Bristol, 29 Oct) and *Novacon* (Buxton, Nov 10-12) looking particularly tasty. *Worldcon* is in China this year (Chengdu, 18-22 October), which is a bit of a trek, but there may be virtual memberships available. Next year's is in Glasgow (Aug 8-12) which should be easier to get to (unless you're in China, I guess). Worldcons are supersized versions of normal cons and worth travelling for.

Outside the UK I'd recommend Boston's *Readercon* (13-16 July), Dublin's *Octocon* (7-8 October) and for something a little more extreme, Atlanta's humungous, cross-genre *DragonCon* (Aug 31-Sep 4).

We have a new anthology out – *From the Depths* is full of tales of the murky deep – mermaids, selkies, pirates sea monsters and all that menacing sea water in your mouth making you cough stuff (buy from us or Amazon). Novels and novellas coming later this year.

This issue we've got time travellers (what would you say to your past self?) a mad tree god (on a pirate ship, of all things) and a detective with a bit of extra spiritual help, plus a sorry tale of AI taking our jobs (very prescient), a dead man walking, a starship running out of air, a dragon that doesn't fly and a gun virus (which would explain a *lot*). In other words, a stimulating mash up of science fiction and fantasy, sometimes edgy, often thoughtful and always entertaining. Enjoy.

Mark

Fugit

Cheryl Sonnier

I first met my future self on a Wednesday.

The day began ordinarily enough. A short bus ride and then up in the lift to the twelfth floor. The workstations on either side of mine were empty. In fact, I was the first to arrive. Other than the woman sitting at my desk.

Her hair was the same length as mine. The same wavy bob, same chestnut colour. I stopped behind her. She sat the same way I did: left forearm on the desk, right hand on the mouse, ankles crossed under the chair.

I was about to tap her on the shoulder and ask what she thought she was playing at, when she said, 'Come on, Helen. How am I supposed to remember what passwords we were using last year?'

That was my voice. I sounded like I smoked forty cigarettes a day, which wasn't fair since I'd never smoked. I spun the chair around.

Screamed.

I hadn't expected the scar. It ran from just under her left eye to the corner of her mouth.

'Hush,' she said. 'It's not that bad.'

'How —'

She gave me a sideways look. 'It's best you don't know. What's our password?'

I crossed my arms. 'How do I know you're really me?'

She rolled her eyes, and I wondered if that annoyed other people as much as it annoyed me. 'When you were thirteen, you had a massive crush on Lucy Fisher.'

My cheeks burned and I looked around to make sure we were still alone in the office. Lucy Fisher. The girl with eyes the colour of a storm at sea, and hair that always managed to look as though she had been ravaged by one. Lucy Fisher. Her rare smile had been a gift from the gods bestowed upon my lowly mortal heart. I had almost forgotten Lucy Fisher. Almost.

And I had never told a living soul.

'Daisy!15.'

My future self raised an eyebrow, and then typed in the password.

Once in, she began writing an email to Lesley, my boss. I read the first line aloud.

'I hereby resign. What? No! You can't do that.' I tried to push her out of the way, but she stayed put. 'I'll lose my job.'

'That's the idea.'

I shoved the swivel chair hard and dived for the keyboard. She rolled backwards towards the next workstation, and I turned my attention to the email. I'd always wanted to tell Lesley exactly what I thought of her management style, but I needed the money for my escape plan. Not that there was ever anything left after Martin got access to my bank account. Future-me lunged and knocked me flying before I could delete the email.

Worse. She pressed send.

I had thirty seconds to undo the action before it was too late., so I shoved her again. She was ready for me this time and as the chair rolled back, she jumped up and tackled me to the floor.

'It's for your own good,' she said. 'Trust me.' She sat on me and short of biting her – which felt wrong, somehow – I couldn't get her off me.

'How can I trust you when you've sabotaged my only income?' What would Martin say? I tried not to think about that.

She sighed and let me up.

'I know it seems drastic but I'm honestly trying to save us from pain and misery. Think about it. Would you really do something terrible to yourself for the sake of it?'

Something on her person beeped and she looked at her smart watch.

'Time's almost up.' She snatched up a pen and notepad from my desk and scribbled something. 'You may as well go straight home. It'll give you more time to pack a bag and go to Mum's. Make sure you take Daisy. Go here tomorrow and tell them you've come for the interview.'

She tore off the sheet of notepaper and pressed it into my hand.

'What... what about Martin?'

'That's why you need to go to Mum's,' she said. "Or Dad's. Anywhere. Just don't be at home when Martin finds out you quit your job.'

I didn't need to ask her why.

'I didn't quit my job. You did.'

She raised an eyebrow. 'I am you.'

I shook my head. I didn't need my own smartarsery beamed back at me right then.

'What's the interview for?' I'd need to prepare, find some practice questions. Maybe if I could get another job quickly enough Martin would be mollified.

'No time to explain.' She held up both hands and I could see through them to the health and safety poster on the wall behind her. 'Molecules don't like to be displaced in time. Until we find a way to stabilise them, we only have about an hour before they snap back to where they came from. Which.' She looked at her watch. 'Is right about now.'

'Will I see you again?'

She shook her head and let go of my hand. 'If you do as you're told, you won't need to. Don't forget Daisy' She gave me a sad little smile and a wave.

I waved back.

Her mouth moved but I couldn't hear any words. And then she was gone. I opened the note to see what she had written. An address down near the Armouries, and the name of a company – Tempus. There was no name of who I was supposed to meet but the time was 9:00 AM Thursday.

At home, I packed a bag with all my clothes, including my interview suit, and a few things I couldn't bear to part with: the pewter jewellery box my sister bought me one Christmas, that held all my favourite broken bits of jewellery; an old photo album with pictures of the family and friends I was no longer allowed to see, and the first edition copy of *Monstrous Regiment* Dad bought me, that I had managed to save from Martin's spite by hiding it behind the bookcase.

Once I'd stashed the bag in the boot of my car, I went back in for Daisy. I strapped her carry case into the front seat, so that she could see me and not be afraid, and stowed the litter box and a bag of her dry food in the boot.

'This is it, girl.' I patted the top of her case and started the car. 'No turning back now.'

I pulled out into the street at the same time as Martin's car stopped at the front of our house. He sat behind the wheel, watching me as I swerved around him and drove away. I didn't dare meet his eyes, so I kept looking ahead as though I hadn't seen him. My knuckles were white by the time I reached the end of the road, and I glanced in the rear-view mirror before turning. He stood unmoving on the pavement, watching.

Mum opened the door and did a double take. To be fair, she tried hard to mask her delight when she saw my bag and Daisy in her travel case, but she didn't quite manage to hide the sparkle in her eyes.

'You've left him then.'

I looked down at my feet. 'Can I stay for a few days?'

She hugged me. 'Stay as long as you want, love.'

I stepped back and put my hands on her shoulders. 'When he realises I'm not coming back, he's going to come looking for me.'

'Let him,' she said. And I wished I had come home sooner. Mum would never have let anyone cut her off from me, no matter what. I felt ashamed then. It had happened slowly but – bit by bit, day by day – Martin had isolated me from everyone I loved. I had told myself I did it for them, to stop him from hurting them too, but at that moment as I looked down into my mother's fierce gaze I knew better. I did it because I was afraid for me.

'Hey,' Mum said, as my eyes welled up. 'Don't. You're home now, that's all that matters.'

By the time I left Mum's flat at 08:00 the next morning, I had convinced myself that I was wasting my time. That whoever Tempus were and whatever they did, they weren't going to employ a woman who knew nothing about them. A search online the night before had yielded nothing. The only reason I had for going was that I had promised myself.

Literally.

Martin was on me before I reached the car, gripping my upper arm as he growled into my ear.

'Where do you think you're going, dolled up like that?'

'Leave me alone, Martin.' I tried to pull away from him.

'*Leave me alone, Martin,*' he mocked in a squeaky voice.

He yanked my arm and strode towards my car, giving me no choice but to follow.

'I have to go back for Daisy,' I said, trying to pull back.

He stopped and I caught my breath. Dare I hope that for once he would be reasonable?

'Do you think I'm stupid?'

I shook my head. 'No, Martin. Of course not.'

'Let your mother keep the cat. Never liked the thing.'

'She'll fret for me.'

'It's a cat, Helen. Get in the car.' He pulled the handle, but the door didn't open. 'Give me the keys.' He grabbed for my bag. I snatched it away.'

'I'm not going with you, Martin.'

He raised his fist, and I closed my eyes, hoping that mum had seen, that she was calling the police right now. If I could stall him long enough, even if it meant him giving me another black eye, it might work this time. There was a shout that sounded like mine. Only I hadn't made a sound. I opened my eyes, and there she was. I was. My future self was on his back, and he was trying to get her off. In the struggle, he let go of me.

'Get in the car,' she said.

He shrugged her off and grabbed her throat. I paused with my hand on the door handle. I should probably have done as she said. Get in the car and drive away while I could. But how could I leave her when she had come back to help me? Maybe this was how she got the scar? I swung my arm with full force and hit Martin on the back with my bag. He left off choking my future self to turn on me. There was confusion in his eyes, and I took advantage of his uncertainty and kicked him in the shin. At the same time, future-me kicked him in the nuts from behind. He fell forward with a grunt, his fist missing me. As he sprawled on the pavement, I darted for the car, grabbing my keys from my bag.

'Quick,' I said. 'Get in.'

I jumped in the driver's side and locked the door. Future me ran around and threw herself in the passenger side. By the time Martin was back on his feet, I had started the engine. He ran towards the car, but I put my foot down and pulled out.

'Thank you,' I said.

She shrugged. 'I had to make sure you didn't go back.'

'The bad thing was Martin?'

'Just drive.' She rubbed her cheek.

That had to be it. Otherwise, why would she come back for me right at that moment? She spent the rest of the journey looking out of the window and ignoring my questions until I pulled up outside Tempus.

'I should be gone when you get back," she said. 'Hopefully, we won't have to do this again.'

'Helen Young?' The receptionist called.

I smoothed my trousers and downed the remains of my coffee in one go, as though to swallow my nerves.

'This way, please.' She took the empty cup and ushered me through a door into a small office.

A woman sat at one side of the desk. Her hair looked as though it was supposed to be in a braid, but wayward strands poked out all over the place. As I approached, she looked up at me with eyes the colour of a storm at sea.

'Helen.' She stood and held out her hand. 'How long has it been?'

I wrapped my fingers around hers. 'Twenty years.'

Lucy Fisher smiled, and the sun came out. I was thirteen again, my hand trembling in hers and my cheeks burning.

The last time I saw my future self, I was on my first trip through time. Instead of going back, Lucy sent me forwards by a few months. I found her in our garden. She still had her scar, although it seemed a little more livid, less faded than the last time I saw her.

'So, it still happens?' I touched the scar, gently. 'No matter what we do?'

'What?' She looked at me as though I'd said something stupid, and I saw my mum looking back at me for a moment. Then she laughed. 'Oh no. It's not this.' She made a pspsps sound and Daisy came running out from under the bench. My future self picked up the cat and nuzzled her, eyes closed.

'Well what then? Why all this?' I asked. Surely, I would have left Martin and found Lucy anyway, without her coming back for me. How else would she have been able to come back in the first place?

'You don't want to know what Martin did to her when I left him,' she said without opening her eyes.

My throat closed. Daisy. My beautiful girl.

'I couldn't bear it, she said. 'I had to come back and put it right.'

'And the scar?' I gestured to her face.

She gave me a sideways look. 'Best you don't know.'

Cheryl Sonnier lives in Leeds with her husband and two cats. She has an MFA in Creative Writing from Manchester Metropolitan University and her short fiction has appeared in Cosmic Roots and Eldritch Shores, Plasma Frequency, Dark Futures, QWF and Roadworks.

WYLDBLOOD
GOTHIC CLASSICS

Gothic masterpieces from H.G Wells, Edgar Allen Poe, Bram Stoker, Robert Louis Stevenson, Henry James, H.P Lovecraft, Edith Wharton and more.

Print and digital download.

www.wyldblood.com/shop,
from Amazon or from bookstores.

Scream of the Firewood

Jonathan Olfert

Drained and chained by wire-hard roots in the guts of a living ship, Hatch Queller fought for clarity. Thirsty roots connected his sword-hand to the nearest of the interwoven, twisted willows that comprised the hull. Blood loss kept him dull enough to feel an empathetic kinship with the tree: he felt sure it didn't want to be here any more than he did. Clots of clinging dirt suggested a natural forest life -- before Harthorne the Anointed, fallen forest god, began to build the living ship that would accompany him into death.

The empathy was clear enough -- the only clear thing in Queller's mind -- that when the nearest contorted willow whispered one night, he fell in love.

"Can you move?" she said in the dark. Roots slid wetly from Queller's veins, unclamped from his sword arm. Other roots from other trees still held his body, but incidentally: he was mostly nourishment for the willow who was speaking. Who was, for some reason, setting him free.

Words refused to take shape. He knotted a fist and let the spike of pain clear his head a little. When he opened it, a hard object settled into his palm: a long piece of unworked stone. "From the causeway outside," the willow whispered. "It took me this long to bring it through the hull."

Far away, Harthorne bellowed a late sermon. The mad tree-god's voice put tension in every root and branch and twisted trunk that comprised the ship. Queller grunted and began sawing.

The sweetness of sap cut through stagnant, blood-fogged air as he applied the sharp rock to the roots that held him. Some of those trees flinched away for, he presumed, their own reasons. Other humans groaned in the gloom. He'd known vaguely that he wasn't the only one ensnared down here, but the ship's root-ribbed belly was a vast and well-fed cavern now. The ship was growing.

Heavy beings -- maybe the corrupted shaghas, the tree-spirits who'd captured him -- shifted on the deck overhead. With effort, Queller kept his feet on the hull of woven roots. He kept the stone spike in hand, poor weapon or not. Stone kept grating on wood, but not of his doing.

The willow, he realized, was sawing herself free.

A curling, starlit stair led up to the deck. That pale light went dim: motion, things approaching. The surface wasn't as even as he'd like; move fast and he'd trip, even in better illumination than this. But his best chance at killing whatever was coming down the stairs was to be at the stairs, so as voices begged for freedom in the gloom, he gave it all the speed he could.

The swordmasters of Crayn had taught him to cross an obstacle-strewn floor in a blindfold. Fighting the fog of blood loss, he shifted forward from stance to stance. His bare feet skimmed the irregular floor in sweeping movements that kept him stable. When he met an obstruction -- a trapped man's leg, a coil of root -- his stance and balance compensated for the halt by muscle memory; he kept moving forward.

The shape coming down the spiral stair was a figure from nightmare: a forest shagha, heavy with old bark and blood-soaked moss, branches clawing up like horns. Queller had killed two like this in a dark glade before two more dragged him down and bound him. Taking care to move quietly, Queller slid around behind the stair.

As the shagha took its last heavy step, Queller jammed the stone spike up into its armpit. The creature wasn't quite animal or plant. The fluid that spurted out was tarry, like a stew of blood and sap. It sloshed against Queller's feet, cooler than blood, and he found he was thirstier than he'd ever been.

The enemy crashed down, splintering and groaning. Even at his full strength, Queller couldn't have silenced that fall. Instead he hurried to search the dead shagha by the starlight coming down the stairs. Like those he'd fought before, up and down the wooded coasts where Harthorne the Anointed ruled, the shagha carried an ancient bronze-headed axe. A useful tool for dominating the wiser trees and keeping humans at bay -- but also an expression of contempt. See how the forest turns your hated axes against you, humans.

Queller took up the axe and leaned against the central column of the stair. Bark shifted under his hand, perhaps in revulsion.

Another shape moved, back the way he'd come. The willow limped into the light. In these forests the line between trees and shaghas was deeply blurred, if there was a line at all. She seemed like both: a sinuous shape of smooth bark, vaguely human-shaped, with hacked-off branches for hair. Deep brown sap, rich with Queller's blood, stained her wherever she'd cut herself free. He suspected she'd left a great deal behind, this being who'd fed on him.

Her remaining leaves rustled with some unknown emotion as she looked down at the dead shagha. Her eyes, deep knotholes, focused on the axe in Queller's hand.

"No hard feelings," Queller rasped. "Not the first time a jailer made prisoners take a chunk off each other."

She relaxed, sagged even, and he got the sense she was as weak as him. "Up quickly," the willow whispered. "Before the stair raises the alarm."

The spiral stair, of course, was much the same kind of being as her. More trusted, maybe, to have earned a place like this in the complex weave of Harthorne's ship. Queller hefted the axe. "Not if he knows what's good for him."

Others called for help. Though Queller was no hero, he hesitated at the base of the silent stair; so did the willow. But up they went.

The ship bobbed in the ocean, alongside a causeway broken by implacable roots. Three masts, all living trees, jutted high against the stars. Sails of barkcloth shivered in the night wind.

The shagha he'd killed had been on guard. The rest of Harthorne's servants clustered on the shore, at the edge of the woods, around a roaring, spitting fire. Harthorne himself stood behind the fire, a shaggy figure nearly as tall as the masts, crowned with branches like antlers. The willow shivered.

Her hands tightened around the ship's rail until it cracked. "Can you hear the firewood?"

The pair of them crept down the ramp. The causeway was an expansion of a natural spit of land whose trees had been uprooted or burned. Out here, the ship's flank and prow blocked the view from Harthorne's massive fire, but it would be a cold walk to the nearest woods. Queller hesitated, unwilling to cross that open space, but equally unenthused about the ocean that surged between the hull and the causeway. At least the surge blotted out the moaning of those trapped inside the ship, and the uncanny sound of the distant fire.

"Can you swim?" he asked.

"Not in saltwater, not wounded." The willow swayed. "I need to take root. You owe me nothing, I can promise you nothing, but will you help me find a place?"

"You'd be kindling by tomorrow." He eyed the nearby hull mistrustfully; it might be listening, even over the sloshing water. "How well do you know the woods here?"

"We're cousins, in your people's terms."

"No, I mean the area."

"Well enough," she said.

Queller sucked his teeth. "Then you're my guide off this coast. Here, take a sip and let's move." He steeled himself and held out his off hand.

The willow stared at him with her knothole eyes. "Don't you worry I could drain you and find my own way?"

"You could've escaped without doing right by me." He set his feet in case his knees wavered. "Go on, drink up."

The willow took his hand, left to left, bark against skin, and placed his palm against her chest, her trunk. Broken shoots stabbed up his tensed-back wrist, cold pricks in the dark.

Five, ten, fifteen heartbeats, and the shoots pulled free. Queller tucked his wrist in his armpit to keep from bleeding more.

The willow shuddered. "I hate the taste. But thank you." She peeled a careful strip from her own arm, a flat length of bark. "For a bandage, and for the pain."

"Good thought." He'd chewed his share of willow-bark after a fight. He knotted the bark over his left wrist; the similar wounds on his right arm had started to close already, despite the effort of killing the forest shagha. "Do you know what they did with my sword and leathers?"

She shook her head, a gentle sway that didn't seem like an imitation of the human gesture. "Do you know the axe?"

"I know my share. Five years a man-at-arms, five more a caravan guard." And another five a cut-rate mercenary and waster of money, aimless, friendless, arguably unpleasant. Truth be told, from the first time he'd stumbled on this fight, on Harthorne's servants and strange ambitions, he'd found more purpose than he'd felt in a lifetime. And he liked the way this axe felt in his sore hands, liked the aggressive balance of the sharply-crooked oak handle and the bronze palstave head. The wrapping at the joint was leather, maybe human leather. Starlight glinted on the deep-carved blade, easily the finest of these axes he'd come across, a masterpiece of ancient work. He gave it an experimental swing and felt abashed when the willow flinched.

The causeway needed cautious footing, all broken stone and the scars where trees used to be. He moved as fast as he dared, past the ship's shadow and into dull light from the fire. Giving the willow more blood might have been a mistake. One stumble, then another, and even after the drink she was barely keeping up.

"We're spotted," she said at his flank. "Hurry, human!"

He gripped the knot of her shoulder to stabilize himself and move her along, and she did the same. They hobbled down the farthest surf-washed rocks of the causeway's edge toward forest that never seemed to get closer. Dark silhouettes jittered against the fire; long shadows cut across their path. By the antler-branches of those silhouettes, he took the enemy for a dozen corrupted forest shaghas like the one he'd killed in the ship's belly. Any one of them was more than a match for him right now, and they moved fast across the uneven ground. Fifty yards, forty, thirty--

"Get in the water," she said. "They'll be on us soon. Swim. I'll root, stay low, close in on myself. Maybe they'll take me for just another stump."

"In these rocks? You'll be driftwood."

"Go," she snapped, and pushed him with the implacable force of a tree bending with a storm.

In better health he might have held his balance. Tonight he didn't have a prayer. He kept hold of the axe, and that was the best he could do. He stumbled down the causeway's far edge and flopped gracelessly into the sea.

Frigid saltwater closed over his head. A deep wave's aftermath pulled him out from the causeway, shockingly fast. He held on to consciousness as hard as he gripped the axe.

He planted a foot on a slippery rock and drove himself up. When his head broke the surface he saw treelike shapes on the causeway, and one of them might have been the willow. Clouds were skidding over the stars. No decent light, not even a gleam on the axe.

Queller washed up more by luck than strength, too cold to shiver and at least a mile down the shore. The dense woods blocked even the smallest glimmer of the fire, but those clouds had come in thick while he was drowning. They glowed a smoldering orange high above the trees. The glow shifted. Perhaps that was Harthorne bending over his fire to turn a human on a spit. A hot meal, to be fair, sounded enviable right now.

Harthorne the Anointed, Harthorne the Hollow, Harthorne of the Rotted Stump: a thousand years old and every bit a bastard. He was dying, folks said, people who'd fled his forests for precarious homes in neighboring lands. Dying and determined to take as much with him as he could. That was the point of the living ship. When it grew to its full stature, Harthorne and his servants and his ship would burn together at the appointed moment. Harthorne's people would sail the seas of the afterlife forever.

That was the plan whispered in refugee camps and roared in firelit sermons, and who but a god could say if it would work.

All that fire sounded most appealing, but even if Queller had the means, he couldn't risk it. He had to assume he was hunted. But warmth was a necessity, or he'd die.

He had, at least, kept hold of the axe. Uphill from the shore, the forest floor was mostly layers of half-rotted pine needles that dimpled under the cover of the trees and buried the lowest branches. He chopped his way in under the boughs of a fat pine, first with energy, then wariness as instinct suggested silence.

Dry branches crunched and snapped, not far away. He bit back a curse and crawled through the half-made aperture. Chopped boughs dug deep and carved hot lines in his back as he forced himself forward.

He nestled in the prickly space down there, curled around the trunk. Many trees here, full shaghas or not, had a vitality, a warmth. He just had to stay awake until he warmed enough to shiver. Then there'd be pain and plenty of it, and he needed to keep silence.

As he waited to hurt, he explored the details of the palstave axe with numb fingers. He traced the designs cast in bronze, the knots of dubious leather, the grain of expertly-chosen oak, the well-worn grip. The axe smelled of sap and blood and fouler things, and now of pine tar, but sweeter, richer. He scrabbled in the dark to place the axe against the trunk, slit the bark, and put his mouth against the tree.

The people of these coasts did that -- customarily and in the camps, at need -- when a tree was more than a tree but not a wakened shagha in its full consciousness. The pine shivered. Its clear sweet bloodsap, untainted by Harthorne's evil or a diet of human blood, came out one slow sip at a time as Queller curled closer to the trunk.

Heavy footsteps stalked outside. He froze, mouth and chest against the trunk, knuckles aching on the axe. If the enemy ripped away the canopy, how quickly could he get to his feet?

Warmth ignited in him, a trickle of stolen life. His fingers found sensation, prickling, then the expected agony.

Once the steps trudged on, he let go of the axe -- an effort -- and tucked tight fists into his armpits as he drank sweet pine-sap. He had no light, no way to mark time, just pain.

Somewhere out there, the beautiful willow was a prisoner, a turncoat, a stump, or just driftwood. He'd left her -- not by choice, but still. That dredged up memories of failures, far too many, things that clawed at his sense of self. Mistakes, crimes, innocent choices whose consequences went sideways. And the faces of the friends and strangers left behind in his wake.

That familiar pain did little to distract him from the agony of survival, but the guilt kept him awake better than the task of drinking. Otherwise he might have passed out at the base of the tree, hidden by its decrepit canopy, sipping sap and spitting bark.

Morning woke him with a frigid breeze that slid through the boughs like a knife between ribs. The wind carried smoke.

"Firewood," he mumbled, and dragged himself out from under the tree that had saved his life.

He was punishingly thirsty -- the bloodsap cloyed in his dry mouth, put an ache to his teeth -- but the forest provided. Over the uneasy thud of his heart, he heard rushing water and lurched off that way with axe in hand. The sound proved to be a simple creek, clear water over stone rather than mud. No doubt a forest's worth of wildlife had pissed in it farther upstream, but he drank his fill, threw it up, drank again. He scrubbed the sea-salt from his body, and the mess of the ship's belly. The effort warmed him despite cold wind and colder water. His clothes were tatters, good for nothing, and he didn't relish the thought of wearing them clammy until they dried, so he stayed naked except for his threadbare braies. His stomach growled and he growled back.

Something else growled too, startlingly close, veiled in evergreens. It shifted out to the bank of the stream on all fours: a forest shagha gone wicked, taller and longer-limbed than the one that he'd killed on the ship. This kind ranged far, harassed and kidnapped. It wore a stinking basket on its back, or maybe the basket was part of it. Stubby branches protruded through sheaves of fungal hair. Its eyes, like the willow's, were empty knotholes.

It straddled the stream carelessly and rose to its full height, a good ten paces, half the size of its master. One wiry hand held a bronze palstave axe larger than Queller's. The other arm terminated in a bloodstained burl the size of Queller's head. Dead bark intergrown with moss had ripped away from huge stretches of smooth underbark. Not weak points exactly, but places where an axe might bite into the hard body that wasn't quite animal, wasn't quite timber.

Five times he'd been this close to a big one. Most often he'd survived those fights -- those much-better-equipped fights -- by taking refuge in a place where it couldn't follow.

He set his feet on the creek bed, water up to his shins, and leveled the axe at its face. If it had words, it saw no particular need to speak.

Its charge came in quick and deceptively high. These kinds of shaghas were accustomed to humans going low, trying to skid or roll under them; more than once he'd seen the big creatures dip low at the last moment and skewer their prey or crush them outright. Queller sank deep on wide-spread feet, pretending to fall for the same gambit.

As the charging shagha swept low with that big axe, Queller leaped clear of the water, got a foot on the bank of the stream, and jumped as high as his sore body would allow. The big head crashed into his chest, almost but not quite strong enough to knock the wind from his lungs; the axe swished under his feet. Vision-inducing, tranquilizing spores puffed from the hairlike mats. By hard-won experience, he held his breath as he gripped the short branch-horns.

The shagha was rising again, to a height where a fall could break Queller's legs. He had time for a chop, just one, to the left side of the shagha's neck, then he swung clear to tumble down a draping pine. Boughs scratched him head to toe, chest and back -- but he landed it. Landed, and faded back into tree cover as the shagha clutched its neck.

It spun his way. That huge burl bashed aside the pine; a single strike from the big axe splintered the trunk. As Queller kept backing up, near-naked and aching, the shagha ripped the pine away entirely, just tore a swath out of the forest, and rushed in.

This time he did go low like the shagha expected -- low, but right in beside the pine's jagged stump. The stump hooked the shagha's arm where it turned into the burl-club. The impact shook the web of pine-roots almost free of the ground, but the stump held.

Flat on his back, Queller got a two-handed grip on his axe and chopped once, twice, at the forearm above him.

Tarry bloodsap sluiced down over his face, chest, arms. As the creature reeled back, Queller scrambled into the trees and swiped its shin with a cut in passing.

It hesitated now. Three wounds, two of them serious, and Queller had cover. It wouldn't charge again. It would slide through the trees if he fled, and if he stood his ground it would batter its way through cover methodically. That was how the big ones fought when they were careful.

Running and standing his ground felt equally unlikely to succeed. It wouldn't underestimate him again.

Here came the shagha and here came the axe, sweeping through intervening saplings. Queller stumbled back between a pair of huge fir trees. The tall shagha paused, then slid between them deliberately, axe-first. Its reeking basket caught on the branches and tore. A stray skull bounced off the intermingled roots of the firs.

A deep roar vibrated in the ground, shuddered in Queller's teeth. The shagha jolted like a man shot with an arrow. The vibration grew stronger. There was a sound like a bursting pumpkin, and a branch jutted through the shagha, then another. The two big firs, matriarchs of the forest, were leaning closer together with the shagha in the middle.

The basket collapsed entirely in a shower of gore. Its carrier came apart moments later, kinetically, like a nut in a cracker. A fresh wave of lukewarm bloodsap drenched Queller, pooled dark in the curls of nearby roots, soaked his shaggy hair and his braies until they clung like a second skin. The fir trees -- shaghas, or something like them -- went still again.

He knelt to scoop up a handful and drank deep. The brown tar tasted like rotten leaves: this creature was none too clean. It burned all the way down.

The corrupted shagha's arm hung twisted from a hatchwork of fir branches. Queller knelt beside its fallen axe, as much to rest as out of reverence for the trees who'd saved him. The shagha had used this weapon one-handed; Queller might manage it with two.

"My thanks, grandmothers," said a familiar voice.

The willow was there, straightening up from a pool of far-flung spatter, tendrils snaking back into her hands. With a smile at Queller, she came closer to the firs and the huge body crushed between them. The pools of bloodsap drained away around her feet. She reached up to touch the dead shagha's contorted arm, and rootlets connected them, draining dark fluid from the corpse. Her broken branches, her weeping-willow hair, sprouted green and shot out to drape in twining waves of thin silver-green leaves. Dried bloodsap flaked away from new scars and clean bark.

The ground shuddered again, not violently but eagerly. The corrupted shagha's body shifted down, somehow, into the ground between and beneath the two firs. Roots seemed to relax. Branches disengaged with a sigh, and stains sluiced away into rough loose bark. The big burl cracked like a chestnut and vanished under a twist of eager roots.

Between the hungers of the willow and the grandmother trees, no trace remained. Queller barely breathed until it was done.

"You lived," he said.

"Just another stump among the rocks." The willow's mouth, or something like a mouth, twisted bitterly. "Just another scar that Harthorne left. They thought only humans broke free, and by the time the ship betrayed me, I was gone. A stand of birch gave me shelter, a place to root and heal." She looked him up and down with empty knothole eyes. "You lived," she said in turn.

"Only because you shoved me in the ocean." Queller mustered a grim smile. "I'm Hatch Queller. Sellsword, you might say."

The willow nodded with a rustle of leaves and twining branches. "Humans called me Sael once, when I gave them shelter in better days."

She touched Queller's arm, and her hard fingers drank up the bloodsap on contact, leaving long clean stripes along his skin. "We should move on," Sael said. "This death will be noticed, and the next time I meet Harthorne, I'd like to choose the hour and the place."

"I have a few thoughts on the subject," he said.

"With me, then?"

The stand of birch admitted Sael readily, but Queller had to leave the axes concealed under a shrub before they'd part for him. From the moment he put the axes down, he was nothing to them. In these forests you never truly knew if a tree was a tree or more, sometimes much more.

A slim creek wound its way through the heart of the birches. On a shore of thick moss, under late-morning light, Sael sank down cross-legged. The day was getting warm for early fall. Queller washed away the bloodsap and lay down in a patch of sun, fingers interlaced behind his head. His body wanted better rest than he'd managed last night, curled up under that low-draped pine. But whatever strength he'd taken from the tall shagha's bloodsap had left him clear, stolen most of his tension, restored what he'd lost by almost freezing to death.

"I'm going to kill Harthorne," he said to the sky, and the birches shivered.

"Are you?" Sael said. "You visitor, you outlander, come to solve our problem?"

"He's my people's problem too, Sael. Hundreds dead, thousands fled." Not that any of it had been his own problem, not until the ship. What had he personally lost to Harthorne before then? Had he been latching onto others' fight in some thirst for stolen purpose?

Probably. Not his first time being a disappointment to himself, though. Not by a mile.

Sael moved over him in a slither of branches. Her weeping-willow canopy enclosed him, made a private space, her wooden face above his, her arms planted at his sides. She breathed, he realized, in a gentler rhythm than a human's, and her breath smelled like a field of wildflowers.

"Harthorne is far beyond you, Hatch Queller, and you don't belong in the ground just yet. But the prisoners on that ship, your people and mine...them, you might save, if you had your strength."

He propped himself up on his elbows, putting them nose to nose. "That sounds like an offer. If you have strength to give, at least."

She laughed. "I saved the life I almost took. We're even."

"I'm well aware. But I wouldn't mind owing *you*."

Sael's uncompromising weight shifted across his thighs, his groin, and he fought to hold still. Knee to toe, she rooted herself in the mossy carpet. She captured his hands in hers and rooted her fingers deep. He couldn't have escaped if he wanted to.

Her mouth was cool bark over firm wood, like kissing a woman in a mask. As he kissed the willow, her neck bent like a pliant sapling, and her canopy flowered bright yellow all around. A wave of heat -- call it magic, call it earth, call it blood -- pressed him deeper into the moss. Green shoots bit into his wrists, his groin, the crease of his thighs, and whether they were drinking or giving life he couldn't say.

"You held back on the ship," he murmured against her mouth. "You could have drank me dry."

"I still might."

Come night, she let Queller leave the birches with the taste of clean sap on his tongue. Stumble, rather, but wide awake and well on his way to focused. He reclaimed the bronze palstave axes from their hiding-place. The lesser one he tucked through the belt of his braies, and the larger one went across his shoulders or served as a heavy walking-stick. He didn't feel the weight. Apart from soreness in various places, he didn't feel much of anything.

A tall shagha stalked the edge of the woods, not far from the causeway and the clearing around Harthorne's cook-fire. Harthorne himself, vaster than anything in sight, sat stoking that fire with a tree-trunk as a poker.

Queller took his time navigating the woods as the sky went from gloomy to black. High clouds obscured the stars. The only light tonight came from Harthorne's fire. He heard screams, or something like screams, and thought of his mental image from earlier, of Harthorne roasting people on a spit -- but no. He was hearing what Sael had heard. He was hearing the firewood.

When the large shagha passed, Queller went low, creeping along the ragged rocks at the edge of the causeway, down where Sael had pushed him into the surf. The ocean tugged at his feet, but with the long axe as his walking-stick, he kept his footing well. When the timing was right, he went up and crossed the causeway -- the ragged ground and stumps, then the broad stretch of broken stone where the ship was docked.

The ship had grown since last night. Prow to stern, it stretched the full length of the causeway. Its ramp was broader and it stank of blood; the whole ship did. Apprehension came on fast and strong. This wasn't the situation he remembered.

Up the ramp anyways, still keeping low. At the top he waited, listened. Toward the prow was the last dull glow of the horizon; to the stern, the fire. He spotted the silhouettes of five roughly human-sized forest shaghas on the top deck, and heard at least one moving down in the belly. Throw in the tall one who'd come from the edge of the woods, and whoever else might come to reinforce, and these were odds as great as he'd ever tackled.

But then again, his blood had never burned like this before.

Down off the edge of the ramp, down to the deck, and the shaghas closed on him like a fist. As if they knew he was coming. Each carried an axe like the one at his belt, or a bronze sword from whatever deep trove had yielded the axeheads. Those swords might not be the equal of good steel, but Queller coveted them on sight.

He swung the larger axe without finesse, a wide sweeping chop at chest height. It crashed into a shagha, tore halfway through the chest, and hooked in deep. The strike drove that shagha into the next one over and hammered both against the rail in a tangle of limbs. As the long axe yanked itself from Queller's hands, now well embedded in whatever passed for a shaga's ribcage and sternum, Queller got in close with the shorter axe and put the second one down in a crush of splinters.

A blow from behind drove him to his knees. Not his first or most painful injury by a mile, but this felt deeply wrong. When he looked down he found an axehead protruding from his chest.

The axe tore free so fast he thought he must have imagined it. His blood felt wrong, too. It flowed slow and cool, it smelled sweet, and rather than fountaining out his life it began to trickle off. And he found that he could stand.

He came up with a bronze sword in hand, a beautiful old carp's tongue suitable for hacking and thrusting. Five shaghas now, one licking his blood from its axe with a tongue like slithering roots. Queller took a shaky breath -- gods, he shouldn't have been able to breathe, not after an axe through the lung -- and settled into a stance hundreds of years more advanced than the bronze sword. The swordmasters of Crayn would spit on him if they knew a fraction of the things he'd done with their teachings, but tonight his stance felt as dignified, as perfect, as it ever had. He raised the tip of the bronze sword and flicked it down in salute.

They came in fast and united, trying to bull him back against the two bodies, back toward the prow and the merciless waves. The bronze sword whirled and hummed.

The last quarter of a carp's tongue blade was narrow for the thrust; the rest was very strong. He bashed the axes into each other, chopped into their oaken grips, or used the narrow point to flick their strikes off-target.

The shaghas drove Queller back - you couldn't avoid losing ground five against one -but Craynite footwork took him easily around the bodies and the mast. He knew he should be dying. Sael -- what she'd given him from herself and from the earth and this cursed forest -- was the reason he lived.

An opening appeared, and a shagha fell to a thrust through the face. And now it was their turn to clamber over the bodies if they wanted to close with him. Queller drew back as if to give an opening, then sprang off his back leg for a thrust that opened a too-eager shagha from wrist to elbow. The shagha's flesh, not quite meat and not quite wood, split like a gutted fish and fountained tarry bloodsap across the deck.

The ship was twisting now, groaning and bucking underfoot. *Turn the ship against itself,* Sael had told him in the sunlit moss among the birches. *It's dozens of my people and of yours, all sewn together. Only some believe in Harthorne. Carry my hope,* he'd thought she said, and hadn't quite understood.

The ship's constituent parts -- trees, shaghas, and everything in between -- were separating, or taking twisted forms to cling to each other, or creaking back into their natural shapes. The deck tore apart and the hull below. The sea fountained up through the gaps and propelled a spray of blood and sap and filth. Queller planted a foot in a shagha's belly and shoved the forest spirit off the edge, into the spray.

The nearest mast was sprouting flowers. Down in the flooded hold, some dark shape was chopping the mast, and being chopped at. The whole ship, Harthorne's vehicle and throne in the afterlife, sighed and settled deeper into the waves. Men and trees smeared with dark things climbed grasping steps, clawed their way to the canted deck. The rail and deck and ramp were coming apart too. All the agonized parts of the ship remembered that because they were alive, they had power.

Queller took their example. As the ship listed and sagged toward the causeway, he left off the fight and jumped, sword in hand. He landed hard, barefoot on broken rock, and felt nothing.

The survivors were leaping from the misshapen hull, clawing their way from the sea, running down the causeway toward the woods. But here came the tall corrupted shagha, the watcher from the treeline, with a bronze blade in one hand and a burl for a fist. It waded into the rush with a great sweep that meshed meat and wood together. Revulsion and indignation settled deep in Queller's gut, and boiled together into fury.

A roar shook the causeway, the trees, the ocean itself. Even Queller and the tall shagha froze, and far too many of the survivors who should have just kept running for the woods. And over by that huge fire, Harthorne was standing. But the corrupted god's mouth was shut, and as he stood, tall as the highest trees, he turned toward the true source of the noise.

A figure lurched from the woods toward the fire. Not as tall as Harthorne, but broader, shapeless, grasping. It seemed made of chains or ropes big enough to anchor the dying ship, and all of that stretched out to snare Harthorne where he stood.

Snare him, and drag him stumbling into his fire.

The firewood screamed revenge, a shrill resonance deep in Queller's bones. The blaze caught the god's hoary bark and spread up past the knees, the hips, the chest. But those chains or ropes were blazing too, and Queller realized with his first true horror of the night that they were the twined branches of a weeping willow.

That was Sael in some transcendent form up there on the shore, trying to burn Harthorne alone. Maybe as a distraction for what Queller was doing, or maybe Queller was the distraction. The tall shagha seemed unsure, and there were others in between here and the fire, fixated instead of killing.

"Sael!" Queller shouted, and broke into a jostling, strong-arm run straight through the survivors. His course crossed theirs: they needed to reach the woods, and he was bound for the fire.

The hacking part of the carp's tongue sword sheared through the tall shagha's spindly leg entirely. It fell fast, hard, and confused, and Queller put the point into its knothole eye as he passed.

The fire was catching; the firewood's agonized rage didn't discriminate. Harthorne staggered and fell to hands and knees, and flame surged up his mossy beard, up Sael's branches. The pair of them -- great shaghas, forest gods unveiled -- were at the fire's mercy and yet they had eyes only for each other. Perhaps they'd been lovers once, rivals, family.

Sael had so much less bulk to her than Harthorne, even in this form. The fire would eat her first. Now Harthorne grabbed a fistful of Sael's corded branches, her smoldering hair, and threw her with a colossal grunt. She smashed against and through the ranks of trees behind.

When Harthorne whirled back to swing her into the heart of the fire, Queller was close enough to matter.

Harthorne's foot was a mass of sprawling roots leading up into a tree-trunk leg. Queller got up on it, gripped the shaggy bark, and hacked at the forest god's shin. Bark came away in grimy chunks and sheets, first charred then slick with gritty brown bloodsap. A good ten yards overhead, wind rushed and branches snapped, punishingly loud. Sael fell with a colossal thud and a dozen split-limb cracks -- but she fell outside the fire.

The effort of swinging her, of throwing her, sent Harthorne down to his knees. Layers of old bark ripped free and Queller went with it. He sprawled at the fire's edge. And now, for the first time, the corrupted god's eyes fell on him.

They weren't like the empty knotholes in the faces of Sael or the shaghas Queller had fought. No, Harthorne had the glossy eyes of a deer to match his vast crown of antler-like branches. An eternity of dried tears stained the corners of his eyes with salt, and all down his wooden face.

He reached down for Queller, stunningly fast. The hand blotted out the forest, blocked every good escape. Queller backstepped into the edge of the fire -- heat stabbed the backs of his legs, his feet -- and rolled through the cinders. Harthorne's fingers thunked deep into ash and earth, far too close for comfort.

Long willow-cords whipped out above Queller's head from the toppled, broken tree that was Sael. Braided branches coiled around Harthorne's wrist by the dozen.

The massive god snorted with audible contempt and yanked. The whole mass of Sael's trunk jolted up and sank back into the ground, biting deep. Her branches whipcracked like broken bowstrings. One lashed Queller across face and chest.

Agony exploded through him; it almost put him on the ground. The axe -- back on the ship -- had merely hurt.

Whatever transformation Sael had sparked in him, being struck by a god's flesh was too much for his body to handle. The carp's tongue sword, edge halfway to irreparable, fell from his nerveless hand.

Instinct shouted. He threw himself aside at the last heartbeat, abandoning the sword. Harthorne's hand caught him a glancing blow that could have caved in a house.

Queller tumbled to a halt in coils of charred branches, splintered roots and burst-open bark: in Sael's embrace. Her face was nowhere he could see, lost in the ruin. Her clear bloodsap was sweet in the air, mingled the scent of wildflowers. No doubt she could regrow if given the chance. No doubt Harthorne would burn her to ash.

Maybe, Queller figured, he'd been an amusement, a distraction for her enemies, a backup plan, a tool. Not bad things to be in a fight like this, for stakes this high, for someone like her and against someone -- he met Harthorne's dark eyes -- like that.

The broken willow-wood shifted around him, and he found himself gripping a straight limb, splintered at one end and burnt at the other. A fire-hardened wooden spear made from -- given from -- the body of a god.

Queller raised the spear above his head.

Harthorne took a step, then paused, as if wary of coming close to Sael. In that pause, Queller dug his feet into the ashy earth and charged. He crossed the intervening ground in heartbeats.

Keep things simple, said the part of his mind still capable of strategy. Don't get fancy or he'll tear you apart.

No leap this time, no tricks, no rolls, no clinging to the tree-god's legs: just an upward stab in passing. The willow spear bit into Harthorne's leg below the knee and tore free.

As Harthorne came around, Queller came in again. Another stab, same knee, this time at the back. Fouled bloodsap sloshed down the side of the god's calf.

Harthorne stomped, and broad roots crushed Queller's foot down into the dirt. Pain surged through his mind, but he knew his business: he was already backing away at a limp, into the trees.

Harthorne paused again rather than follow, and Queller thought of the two grandmother firs who'd saved him. Harthorne might be as tall as the highest trees in these woods, and bulkier than any of them, but how many might turn against him, seeing what they'd seen tonight and tasted on the wind? There wasn't a corrupted shagha in sight, nor a survivor. The forest teemed with life tonight; it echoed with triumphs and tragedies. The ship, Harthorne's great work, was gone. All he had left was his fire, and that fire, untended, was burning down to a smolder.

Queller could almost -- almost -- feel sympathy for the god. Instead he took a running step and threw.

At this range with a good arm behind it, even a crude spear could fly true. The fire-hardened point struck Harthorne with a hollow thunk, in the part of his trunk that would have been his gut if he were human. Charred bark kept the spear from glancing off, but wasn't dense enough to absorb the blow. The spear bit deep.

What spilled out bore no resemblance to shagha bloodsap as Queller knew it, not even the corrupted kind that stained Harthorne in a dozen places. This was pale slop, fetid and writhing, dotted with chunks of rotten wood. Harthorne the Hollow, some called him; Harthorne of the Rotted Stump. The latter name had come with a fanciful mental image of a tree-god tearing himself from his stump to walk the earth, but Harthorne was the stump himself, wasn't he, a ruin of a tree, soft inside and half-consumed.

The pale stinking mess, streaked with gritty bloodsap, rolled down Harthorn's legs and sizzled on the ground. Harthorne swayed in a cold wind off the sea. His highest antler-branches cracked, and Queller backed up fast as spiral-fractured deadwood thunked into the dirt.

One giant hand swiped feebly at the spear. It tore free with a shield-sized patch of bark, rotten inside and out, and another surge of fishbelly-colored slime. Harthorne's knees hit the ground, then his face and antler crown: a double earthquake. An exultant cry rang in the back of Queller's head, all weak and wounded voices, the last of the firewood united in triumph.

At the edge of the dying fire he found a half-burned log almost too big to lift: Harthorne's poker. Queller put his arms around it and heaved. The narrow, blackened end pivoted around, trailing sparks, and its embers came to rest in the fallen god's crown. Lichenous bark and tattered things caught flame almost at once. Harthorne struggled weakly, lurching like a wagon in mud, as Queller lit the god's head on fire.

Pale rot slicked the fallen spear. He picked it up anyway and, without ceremony, jammed it into Harthorne's neck. Blood and filth hissed in the firepit.

In a night of vast movements, great rushing sounds still had the power to startle him. He flinched as the broken thing that had been Sael dragged itself forward. Roots latched onto Harthorn's flaming skull and drank deep.

Split limbs creaked and took new forms, smooth and graceful. Harthorn's crown of antler-like branches ripped free and grafted itself above a face Queller knew fondly and well.

As she rose taller than ever, draped in majestic silver-green, he thought of how he'd felt such affinity with Sael -- loved her, in hindsight -- when he first heard her voice in the dark. He wondered how someone so glorious had become just another prisoner woven into the ship. He outright wept to think that she could have been forced to feed on any random captive, rather than someone who could help her become this god. Now on his knees in worship, he marveled at his luck: the man who'd shared blood with the willow.

Jonathan Olfert is a neurodivergent fantasy, sci-fi, horror, and paleofiction writer. Some of his stories can or will be found in Beneath Ceaseless Skies, Interzone, and Lightspeed. He and his partner live near Halifax, Nova Scotia.

Unfamiliar

Matt McHugh

The body was still in place in the alley. A woman. Forties, maybe. It was hard to tell with all the head trauma. She was fully clothed, hands and feet bound with plastic zipcord, mouth covered with surgical tape. Nostrils left exposed. There was a harness of nylon straps around her torso.

"Ms. Gellar?" A man approached me. Middle aged. Tall, bad posture. Stiff suit and mono-color tie, the frumpy paternalism that screamed plainclothes. "I'm Detective Sullivan. Thank you for coming."

He shook my hand. His grip was firm but not dominating, his face haggard but not hostile. There was a weariness about him, except for the way his eyes narrowed keenly, as if to take in everything and betray nothing. I found myself with a reflex to match his demeanor.

"Martine Gellar," I replied. "What happened?"

He pointed up. "Fourth floor fire escape. Fibers from the straps were found in an overhead railing that appears to have given way."

"The death was accidental?"

"There's a theory she was dangled over the edge, with an intent to scare rather than kill."

"And what do you think?"

He shrugged. "Mmm."

I needed no special perceptions to sense all the speculation behind that shrug. "What can I do for you, Detective?"

He nudged me back, out of earshot of the scene workers.

"The victim was Nidra Samejo. Did you know her?"

I failed to keep a reaction from my face, a small gasp from passing my lips. "Mostly by reputation," I answered, trying to reclaim my stoicism. "I met her once at a lecture a few years ago."

Nidra Samejo was an icon, the one who most helped to convince the world—and frightened people like me—that we were not insane. I could see her on stage, holding hundreds spellbound. Afterward, I waited two hours in a book-signing queue. The way her face brightened when I told her what I did. She thanked me. Took my hand in both of hers. I felt the memory of their warmth. Those hands now bound bloodless by zipcord.

"You think this had to do with her work? An attack by protesters?" I spoke gruffly, again trying to suppress any appearance of emotion. But inside… inside I was reeling.

"You tell me," said Detective Sullivan. He hesitated, gesturing vaguely. "Can you see anything with your, uh—"

I tensed up, dreading what might come.

"Your, uh, partner," he said at last.

I relaxed, relieved not to hear "spook" or "shade" or one of the usual slurs.

"I prefer the term 'Familiar'," I said.

He nodded, held up his hands in deference. He took a step back. I wondered what he thought I was going to do.

I closed my eyes—because sometimes that does help—and felt around for Edgar. There's a current fad among scientific types to frown on giving a name or gender to a Familiar, but most sensitives I've ever met do it, and certainly all the bonded. He's been "Edgar" to me for twenty years, since I first became aware of him when I was twelve. I don't know why, but it felt right. What do scientists know about it anyway?

I found him in one of the nearby buildings, eavesdropping on a husband and wife screaming in anger at each other. He was often drawn to things like that.

I called to him. He heard, but drifted further away, like a child avoiding a parent. That metaphor—parent and child—had become more common in the literature of Familiars lately. I don't like it. He's not my child. He's my… something else.

Edgar. I summoned a body memory of bonding with him. *Come to me. I need you.*

He came. As he approached, I saw through his vision. That's not quite right, but it's hard to describe any other way. Through his perception, I can sometimes recognize objects. Sort of how, in a dream, that doesn't look like your house but you know it is. I saw the alley, the body (Edgar has a fascination with corpses), then myself, waiting for him.

We connect. I feel him surround me, fill me.

I've often been asked what it's like. The best comparison is submerging, lowering your body underwater. No, not under, but rather water rising and engulfing you. Like the entire world floods, but you can still breathe. I've always been afraid of water, of drowning. Never even learned to swim as a child. But with Edgar in me, it's like I'm walking on the ocean floor, perfectly at home.

I explain to Edgar—with the wordless communion I could never explain to anyone who hasn't experienced it—that there's been a death and what I need him to do. He understands. We've been through this together many times, though lately he's more distracted, harder to focus. He just wants to play. I can feel his desire moving within my body, tingling on my skin. *Later*, I say. *Right now, I need you to look. Please.*

It takes a little pleading, but Edgar soon gives in. He leaves me—I feel him like warmth rushing out of the top of my head—and hovers by the fourth floor fire escape. I nudge Edgar past two scene workers and into the apartment. I can feel the layout of the room, the position of walls and furniture. The door is intact, unforced. There's nothing to indicate struggle or ransacking.

Now, I push Edgar further, casting about for residuals. In places where someone has experienced intense fear or pain, those sentiments linger. Like a scent, an echo. Edgar can pick up remnants of those emotions, and pass them to me. It can be the most satisfying aspect of our partnership. Sometimes, the most horrific.

They are incredibly strong, perhaps the strongest I have ever felt. It shouldn't surprise me. Samejo had the most advanced bond with a Familiar yet measured, amplifying her emotional aura. I felt it when I was in her presence years ago. Even now, as fading residuals, her imprint was overwhelming.

Samejo suffered greatly in that apartment. It comes to me through Edgar's perception like a putrid aftertaste. But not at first. Other memories still lingered in the room. I can feel her opening the door, letting someone in. A man. He is known to her. I can see his shirt, his jacket.

I can't make out his face.

It is blurred over, obscured in the traces of her memory. I push Edgar to focus, but the residuals are already evaporating, as they do for all the dead. Despite their strength, the final moments of Nidra Samejo dissolve like a misty handprint on glass.

I opened my eyes to find Detective Sullivan staring, his dour face changed, intrigued and repelled in equal measure.

"Did you see anything?" he asked.

"The man who attacked her," I said. "She knew him."

"Who? Who was he?"

I struggled to reply, to make sense of what I'd witnessed.

"She recognized him. That was clear. But his face, her understanding of how she knew him, it was… missing. As if erased from the impressions left by her memory."

"Is that possible?" he asked.

"I've never encountered it before. But, frankly, it's different every time."

"And what about her Familiar?"

Samejo had a legendary Familiar. Castillo, she called it. She joked he was her hot-blooded Latin lover. I felt nothing of him now. Not the slightest hint.

"It's gone," I said to Detective Sullivan.

He frowned. Knit his brow. But made no sound beyond a cryptic, "Hm."

At the precinct, Sullivan offered me coffee, poured himself a cup of water. "This is all my acid reflux can handle anymore," he said.

"Edgar would never let me give up caffeine," I said. When I saw his perplexed expression, I added. "My Familiar. That's what I call him. He has something of an addictive personality."

"He feels what your body feels?" asked Sullivan.

"Exactly. Familiars have no material body, so they're drawn to people like me, who are sensitive to their presence. It's how they connect to the physical world. Researchers have confirmed the electromagnetic fields they generate change when a human they've bonded to experiences pain, pleasure, sadness, euphoria, what have you. They partake in what we feel. In return, we experience what they perceive with senses completely different from our own."

"And that includes… um," Sullivan tapped his forehead.

"To a degree, yes," I replied. "Electrical activity in the brain can be sensed by Familiars. People think it's mind-reading. It isn't. It's more like the general tone of someone's mental state gets broadcast, and Familiars can pick it up."

"How's that work with dead people?"

"Very intense feelings are strong enough to leave a residue that persists for a short time. If I get to a murder scene soon enough, my Familiar can perceive the impressions left by a victim."

"It's like the old myth that an image of your killer gets captured in your eye."

"Sort of," I replied.

"And how many people do what you do?" asked Sullivan. "Use a relationship with a Familiar to solve criminal cases?"

"I've heard of a few that help locate missing persons, but—officially working on homicides—I'm the only one I know of."

"That's why I called you," he said, tightening one side of his mouth, the first semblance of a smile I'd seen from him. He laid a tablet on the table between us, flipped through screens of reports.

"These are complaints by people with Familiars over the last two years. Threats, stalking, from haters and fanatics alike. Hundreds of cases. Given the tiny percentage of the population confirmed to have a Familiar—one in a hundred-thousand, last I heard—that's a lot of harassment."

"You don't have to tell me."

"And it's on the rise. More religious and political groups pushing for legislation. Protests, demonstrations, online hate groups. And, on the other side, people rallying to these cults." He looked up sharply. "I'm sorry. That's a rude term."

"But not an incorrect one," I said. "People flock to us. For good and bad reasons. A few have really damaged our reputations by exploiting it." I ease into the next line, careful not to choke up. "That's why Nidra Samejo was so important to us. She spoke openly of what the human race has whispered about for centuries: we share this world with invisible beings. She endured the hatred and the mockery, was honest about the advantages of bonding, and the toll it

takes. She worked with scientists studying the phenomenon. A lot of what's been verified—facts that can no longer be dismissed as hysteria or superstition—came from what she started."

"And she was killed because of it."

Sullivan may as well have punched me in the gut on that one. He obviously saw my distress, reached out and placed his hand on mine.

"I've been a detective a long time," he said. "Grief. Anger. Disgust. They don't go away. You compartmentalize so you can do the job, but you never lose them. You shouldn't. They're motivation. Ms. Gellar, I asked for you on this case because I believed you would be especially motivated."

When your Familiar can sense hidden deceptions, you quickly learn no one is ever quite what they appear to be. It's made me shrink from flesh-and-blood connections, taught me to embrace distrust. Right now, I sensed nothing but clarity from Detective Sullivan, as if his aura were a sheet of smooth white paper. It surprised me how much I wanted to trust him.

I let him see me wipe away the beginnings of tears.

"Then let's get to work," I said.

Back in my apartment, I looked over the reports Sullivan shared with me. They told me things I already knew, but they were still distressing.

Pages and pages of hate speech from online forums, emails, private messages. Rambling public invective from pundits, televangelists, politicians. All the usual talking points: it's a hoax; it's satanism; it's an alien invasion; it's a bunch of sad, lonely women desperate for attention. The illiterate venomous attacks were easier to take than the articulate arguments filled with warped facts and fear-mongering. It's very easy to make frightened people hate us.

I set down the reports, tried to put them from my mind. I closed my eyes and reached out to Edgar. I found him buzzing the neighboring rooftops, peering into skylights. I called him, sensing as he passed through walls and floors until he rushed into me. I wanted comfort but Edgar was fidgety, playful. I felt the tug, the peculiar prodding he does when he wants whiskey. I'd been drinking far too much lately and pushed back. I ate a few chocolates to distract him. Edgar prefers Ghirardelli but will tolerate Hershey's. He settled a bit but soon began to nudge again. He kept looking over, pulling me toward the nightstand. I sighed and opened the drawer, took out a vibrator.

"Is this what you want?"

Edgar squirmed within me. Fine. I wasn't going to sleep anyway without some distraction. I turned it on and let it slide down.

"Here you go, buddy."

Detective Sullivan called and woke me mid-morning.

"There's some leads I wanted to run down," he said. "Can you come with me?"

Half an hour and two espressos later, I was waiting outside my corner hipster coffee bar when he pulled up in a beige juggernaut of a sedan.

Downtown, on narrow Tribeca streets snarled by tunnel traffic, Sullivan parked in front of a fire hydrant and pressed the buzzer of a door stenciled *The Temple of Invisible Light*. I'd heard of it. An operation run by someone who claimed to have a Familiar but refused to submit to any scientific verification.

The Temple was a rented office space over a bodega with a warren of messy cubicles up front, a mysterious closed door on the back wall. A receptionist informed us that the founder, someone named Alastair Woodley, was not available but produced the "Executive Secretary," a middle-aged woman who eyed us distrustfully and introduced herself as Sister Colleen Fisk.

The news of Samejo's death hadn't yet started to spread, so I got to see her face as she heard.

"Oh no!" said Fisk. "Such a blow to all of us."

Her face mimed anguish, but the tone of her thoughts—the peculiar aura of color and vibration Edgar relayed to me— suggested there was no real grief.

"Do you know if your founder ever met her?" asked Sullivan.

"No, I don't think Father Alastair ever did."

He held out his phone, queued and ready, and played a video of Alastair Woodley and Samejo on a podcast, sitting across from each other, cross-arguing into microphones. Samejo counted on her fingers points that proved Woodley to be a fraud.

"That was two years ago," he said. "Do you know if it had any impact or donations or enrollment?"

"I have no idea. It's not something we fret about."

Fisk smiled tightly. She radiated subterfuge like a thicket of dark fractals.

"Is there anything else I can help you with?" she said.

"You tell me," said Sullivan. "We're investigating the murder of someone who denigrated your founding father. There's nothing else you have to say about that?"

Fisk's aura went icy, knots of congealed blue threaded with peppery veins of anger.

"People think they know everything," she said. "But this universe is so much bigger than we than we can imagine. It's sad so many are threatened by that. It's small. And I choose not to be small."

The next stop was just a few blocks away, but a polar opposite from The Temple of Invisible Light. The Church of Christ's Ministry was an evangelical group committed to—according to their online profile—"purging the Earth of invisible demons." At least they agreed on one point.

Our reception was simultaneously more courteous and more hostile. Pastor Reverend Lee-Kwon Park, Master of Divinity and Certified Spiritual Life Coach, bowed and smiled and told us all who consorted with Familiars were going to Hell.

"Why is that, Reverend Park?"

"Because these creatures are not part of the natural order as God intended it. They're violations, perversions that prey upon the spiritual void of desperate people. Ms. Samejo helped usher demons into this world. I'm glad she can do that no longer."

"You do realize you're talking about someone who was murdered yesterday?"

"I do. And I mourn for her," he replied. "She is in the grasp of perdition, now and for eternity. I would have liked the chance to save her soul."

Again, Sullivan held up his phone. Scrolled through pages of text. "You wrote a lot on your blog about how evil she was." He quoted passages. "'Nidra Samejo is doing the Devil's work.' 'Her followers are as misguided as those pledged to any death cult.' 'She even chooses the word "familiar," invoking the folklore of witchcraft and satanism.' Do you stand by those statements?"

"Every one," he answered. I wish death on no one, but make no mistake: we are fighting a war. A battle for the souls of our children. These people who claim to bond with these demon-familiars… you do realize they're mostly vulnerable young women? Victims of neglect or abuse, addiction or mental illness. And one day they hear a voice in their heads telling them they're special. They're unique and powerful, and the rest of the world is wrong. That's the seduction fallen angels offer. The Serpent in the Garden. The oldest story of all. I am sorry Ms. Samejo was murdered, but I'm glad she can no longer help the enemy—even if she never understood that's what she was doing."

Park's vibrations were calm, like waves in a grassy field stirred by a gentle breeze. If he were taking a polygraph, his lines would be flat as the horizon.

Outside, Sullivan said to me, "Are you alright?"

I nodded. "It's nothing I haven't heard before."

He pointed to a diner. "I could use a sandwich. Can I get you something?"

"Coffee would be lovely. And a cinnamon roll. Edgar could use some sugar."

Sitting in a booth, Sullivan got a message and frowned at his phone.

"Preliminary forensics," he said. "It's likely Samejo was alive when she hit the ground. No drugs. No asphyxiation. No trauma that couldn't be explained by a forty-foot drop onto concrete. Still no useful physical evidence from the apartment. And it says here her binding was done quote-unquote skillfully, using bowline and clove hitch knots designed to hold but not overtighten."

"So we're looking for a sailor," I said. "Or maybe a boy scout?"

Sullivan released the tiniest of chuckle-snorts. "Look at this," he said, showing me the screen.

It was a photo of a bulky rubber wedge and tube, apparently bearing teeth marks.

"Is that a bite guard?" I asked.

"Uh huh. Like the kind used in electroconvulsive therapy. Keeps you from chipping your teeth or severing tongue, with a passage so you can breathe. Do you think I could force that into your mouth?"

"Not on the first date," I said. That got an actual chuckle. I felt honored.

"Quite a job to get that in when someone's struggling for their life. What does that suggest to you?"

"She put it in willingly."

Sullivan replied with his most understated "Hm."

"I'd like to go back to the scene," I said.

"Do you want company?" he asked.

I took it as sincere, protective, but when I'm working with Edgar, I have no patience for gawkers. The way Sullivan had stared at me before, with fascination and revulsion... the way so many people do. I didn't want to see that on his face again.

"I'd prefer to be alone."

Sullivan nodded and called in the request.

When I got to Samejo's apartment, a pair of techs were still working. They made me wear me booties and gloves, but otherwise let me be. As I figured, there were no more lingering impressions. I looked out the window to Samejo's fire escape.

"Can I go out?"

He lifted the window for me, steadied my elbow as I ducked low and stepped through.

I looked down. The height was dizzying, the drop sickening to contemplate. I looked overhead. There was an angled bracket on the balcony above me. Black-and-yellow forensic tape framed a spot where a weld had pulled apart.

I went back inside the window—again, the tech gave me a hand through the awkward duck and climb.

"Have you found her phone? Computer? Tablet?" I asked.

"Not yet." answer the tech.

"No lobby or doorbell camera?"

"Had a piece of tape over it."

"Fingerprints on the tape?"

"They were hers."

"She taped over her own door camera?"

"So it seems."

I looked out to the fire escape again. It would be awfully hard to wrangle a bound, struggling person through the narrow window. Much easier to tie up the victim on the balcony. A victim who crawled out voluntarily, put in a mouth guard, taped over her door cam, and let herself be hoisted and hung.

Nidra Samejo didn't just know her killer. She helped him.

I called Detective Sullivan. Told him what I thought.

"We've identified some known contacts," he said. "Do you want to be present for the questioning?"

"Very much so."

"You understand any impressions you get from your, uh, Familiar are not admissible. You'd just be consulting."

"I understand. I still want to participate."

"I'll send you an interrogation schedule when we have it. What are you going to do now?"

"I've had enough for the day," I said. "I'm going home."

"Do you want me to send an escort?"

"I'll be fine, Detective Sullivan. Goodnight."

"Goodnight, Ms. Gellar."

I was walking through a subway transfer tunnel, when I noticed I was being followed.

I didn't get a look at the face, but there was no doubt someone—male, caucasian—got on when I did, changed cars when I did, then followed me through a turnstile.

I sent Edgar to check him out, and got the unmistakable vibe of vigilance, someone glancing up to keep track of me, checking around to see who was watching him.

I went above ground and took a few false turns. He stayed right with me. I walked along the edge of a closed playground, leading him toward a building where I used to live. I stepped behind the courtyard wall and waited. Edgar shadowed every step of my pursuer, tracking him like radar. I could see him and myself as if we were dots on a video-game maze, one steadily closing the distance. Just as he reached the corner, I had Edgar intrude into the man's brain, triggering that moment of vertigo unique to the rush of a Familiar. When he paused to shake his head, I stepped around the corner.

From my mandatory defense classes as a police consultant, one thing the instructor had said always stuck with me: When you go for the balls, go big. Most good body targets—bridge of the nose, solar plexus, eyes—require precision. Testicles are different. You can't see them. They shift around. So, when you go for them, use something broad. Flat of the palm, rather than knuckles. Forearm or instep of the foot. Or, my personal favorite: good old thigh. Step parallel to

his foot, raise up your knee, and blammo. Works like a charm. Especially when you have a Familiar setting him up for you.

Down he went. I took two big steps back, watching to see if he'd get up. When he continued to writhe and moan, I was about to turn and run when I heard,

"Martine! Wait!"

I stopped. Turned back. I stared as the man lifted his head, looked at me with watery eyes.

"Jimmy?" I said.

He nodded. Grimaced. "Jesus fuck, what did you do that for!"

"I didn't know who you were!" I took his elbow, helped him up, leaning against the wall. "Why are you following me like that?"

"I was trying to get in touch with you!" he said, wincing pathetically. "Looking for a discreet place to make contact. You know… like you fucking asked!"

"I'm sorry, Jimmy. I just didn't think… oh, god, I'm sorry."

"Whatever. Anway, our mutual friend needs your help," he said, starting to sound more himself.

"I'm working a case right now," I answered. "I can't get involved."

"It's important," said Jimmy. "A big one. Big commission. It has to be tonight." He held out an envelope. "Here. Be there at nine o'clock."

He turned and limped away. After a few dozen paces, he slowly straightened up. I heard him yell, "Fuck!" one more time for good measure.

Inside the envelope was a wrapped bundle of twenty dollar bills. It looked like more than the usual thousand-dollar fish-hook. A sticky note had the address of an upscale restaurant not far from my apartment. I had just enough time to go home, change, and get there by nine, if I hurried.

When I arrived, Jimmy was waiting at the bar. He'd cleaned up and, like me, was dressed respectably in semi-formal evening wear. He stood from the stool—without difficulty, I was pleased to note—and embraced me with a friendly kiss.

"Sorry about before," I whispered as we hugged.

"Don't remind me," he said bitterly, then drew back with a radiant smile and escorted me to a table.

We ordered appetizers and expensive wine, chatted about casual nothings, until Jimmy lowered his eyes and said softly, "They just walked in."

"Who?"

"A Brazilian banker and the local developer they've been working with. The plan is to demolish some old brownstones near the Seaport and put in a luxury hotel. They claim they've got tacit approval from city zoning, but there's historic sites in the area that could have an impact on cost and schedule."

"What's the big deal?" I asked. "Aren't delays and cost overruns inevitable in construction?"

Jimmy took a sip of wine, gave a small chuckle as camouflage.

"Our mutual friend has some other parties interested," he said. "Including at the state gaming commission. This could be the first true casino within city limits."

"Really? Gambling in Manhattan?"

"Keep your voice down," Jimmy said as he flipped through the menu. "There's a lot at stake here so we need to know if they're lying about the zoning approval. Ah, right on schedule. The big guy just walked in."

I fought the temptation to turn around. I knew Jimmy was speaking about the secretive businessman who, over the last few years, had paid me to use

Edgar to gather information. We'd never met—Jimmy managed all our contact—though I'd caught a glimpse of him. I didn't recognize him. Just another old, rich white guy to me, but one shrewd enough to realize a Familiar could be used for industrial espionage. Edgar and I had inspected building foundations, peeked inside locked warehouses, and followed rival investors to their mistresses. For that, I was paid on the sly. Once a month, I went to a university campus, answered a few questions, and ten-thousand dollars—after taxes—showed up in my bank account as a "research stipend." Works for me.

Jimmy slid an earphone across the table. I slipped it in and listened as my benefactor chatted with his unsuspecting partners.

"Can you hear?" asked Jimmy.

I pretended to look at the menu and nodded.

"Ok, so during the course of dinner, we need to know how they react when certain things are mentioned."

I felt around for Edgar, who was sniffing through the thoughts of patrons in the crowded restaurant like a dog looking for scraps. I called him, struggled for a bit to wrangle his interest, then directed him toward the men at the table a few rows behind my back.

One man was older. He had an air of worldliness, of confidence and caution. The other was young, humming with anxiety covered up with bravado. I could hear them in my earpiece as I felt the impressions Edgar sensed.

Jimmy and I ordered and ate—a counterfeit couple having dinner—as I tried to follow the conversation behind me. Most of it was excruciatingly dull. Interest rates. Union negotiations. The cost of reinforced concrete. It was hard to stay focused, let alone keep Edgar from wandering off.

"OK, now," said Jimmy, out-of-the blue. "Pay attention."

"But none of this matters," I heard our employer say, "unless we can break ground by March of next year. And that means demolition, utilities, roadwork, detours—the city has to sign off on all of that. You can guarantee they will?"

"Absolutely," said the young voice. "Everything is lined up." I could feel him as he spoke, Edgar passing through his thoughts like a sunbeam that highlighted all kinds of dusty swirls and eddies where there should have been a smooth flow. It was obvious to me.

"He's lying," I said.

"You're sure?" asked Jimmy.

"Yes, no problem," the older voice at the table added. "I've got half the downtown zoning committee in my palm, all set to sign off on the variances."

"Him, too." I said. "He's less obvious, a much better liar, but, yes, I'm sure about both."

"Great," said Jimmy. "All we needed to know." He flagged a waiter. "Check, please?"

Jimmy paid, we left quickly, and walked arm in arm a few blocks until Jimmy disengaged and said, "Alright, thanks again."

"That's it?"

"That's it. Our mutual employer suspected as much and just wanted confirmation. We got what we needed from you."

"OK then," I replied, feeling oddly deflated, as if this were the beginnings of a break-up. "Sorry about before," I added pointing to his crotch. "You want me to kiss it and make it better?"

"Ha. Not even if I swung that way. Not into the whole spook menage et trois

thing. I'll be in touch when we need you again."

And he walked away.

When I got home, Edgar was needy, but I was in no mood. I drank most of a bottle of wine and took a non-opioid, prescription tranquilizer. As I drifted off, I felt Edgar sniffing around the couple down the hall just starting to engage in foreplay.

I woke some twelve hours later to my phone ringing. It was Sullivan.

"We have Samejo's brother at the station for questioning. If you're available, I'd like you to come."

I got there as soon as I could, using a brisk walk to clear my head. Amit Samejo was in an interrogation room—he'd come voluntarily—looking heartbroken. Sullivan introduced me as "Detective Gellar" and said we just had a few more questions.

"What did you think of your sister's work?" he asked.

"You mean with the ghosts?" replied Samejo. "To be honest, I never liked it. I guess I never understood it."

"Were you ashamed of her?"

"I actually went to a few of her lectures," said Samejo. "Morbid curiosity, I suppose. But when I saw her in front of hundreds, spellbound by her every word, I was in awe. She was older than me, always smarter. When she was fourteen, I saw her change. When this... spirit—or whatever you want to call it—came over her. As she got older, began to write and lecture about the whole thing, I didn't know what to make of it. Maybe I was proud and ashamed at the same time."

Amit Samejo began to weep.

"Were you jealous?" asked Sullivan.

"No."

"Did you want her to stop? Did you ever wish she could just be normal?"

"Many times."

"Did you believe she was possessed by a demon?"

"No."

Sullivan slid a tablet screen over to Samejo. "That's a thread on an online forum discussing one of your sister's lectures. You replied to a comment saying, quote, 'It's lovely that all you are so enthusiastic about being possessed by demons.' Did you post that?"

"That was over ten years ago."

"Did you post it?"

"I was upset. Before I appreciated what my sister was doing. God, doesn't anything ever go away online?"

"Is that what you thought? That your sister was possessed by a demon?"

Amit Samejo was quiet, staring directly at me.

"She's one of them, isn't she?" he said.

I glanced at Sullivan. He just gave a small nod.

"I have a partnership with a Familiar, yes," I replied.

"A partnership?" he asked. "Is it something you chose, or something that was forced upon you? Does it make you feel powerful, being bound to a shadow? Or despair, knowing you will never again have privacy?"

"Like many things in life, it has benefits and compromises."

"Well, then, here's a benefit to me," said Samejo. "None of this interview is admissible because of your presence so I can say whatever I like. I knew and loved my sister. I watched her struggle with something I couldn't understand, and come out stronger for it. I know nothing about you. Except that you're a ghost whore who spies for the police. Now, I'd like to go. Do I need to call my lawyer to make it happen?"

After a few more questions, Samejo was released. He said nothing further to me, giving me one contemptuous glance as he left the station.

"Are you alright?" asked Sullivan.

"I've been called worse," I replied. But I was shaken. This man, who loved his sister in spite of her status, hated me for the same thing.

"What did you think? About his honesty."

"I'm not a human lie detector," I said, more sharply than I wanted. "I can perceive some things you can't, but I can't read minds. His grief is real. I'm sure you can see it, in his face and body language. And his anger. It's overwhelming. It's hard to see beyond it."

"I get that, too," said Sullivan. "I believe he cared for his sister. I wonder if he cared enough to try to set her free."

He nudged me toward a private corner and took out his phone. He fiddled for a moment, then showed me a still frame of Nidra Samejo looking into camera. He tapped the video play.

"More and more I've come to feel his invasiveness," Samejo said on the video. *"He never leaves me alone, resists what I ask him to do, pushes me to do what he wants. It's exhausting. Disturbing sometimes. He has constant... appetites. Stronger, more demanding. I have trouble telling what's him and what's me. I need him back off, but he won't. Is this just a phase? Or is it the way things will be from now on? Will everyone with a Familiar have to deal with this? We've been through a lot, some difficult transformations. Maybe we'll get through this. But I have to admit, I'm worried."*

"That's from a private vlog Samejo was keeping for a research study. She'd done it for years, but a few months ago, entries like this started—even though, in public, she was as upbeat as ever."

Sullivan looked me up and down, his face bearing an expression I preferred not to see.

He continued. "Investigators looking through speeches and interviews found her mention a few times a fear of heights. Being tied up and dangled from a balcony would be pretty intense for her."

"What are you saying?" I asked.

"You said Familiars feel what their host feels," he replied. "What if you wanted to punish your Familiar? Make them feel something unpleasant. You'd have to feel it yourself, wouldn't you? And what if you needed help to do it? Who would you turn to?"

Back at my apartment I, once again, drank too much, ate too much, and sat around in a funk as Edgar nibbled at my edges. I counted the envelope cash from Jimmy ($1600) and thought about how I'd spend it, since it was too big an amount to deposit. I put on an old favorite romantic comedy and let Edgar enjoy my honest laughter at jokes I'd forgotten. I was drifting in and out on my couch when, again, my phone woke me.

"Ms. Gellar? Detective Sullivan. Sorry to call so late. Amit Samejo just turned himself in. We have him in holding, but he says he wants to speak to you before giving a statement."

"I'll be there in twenty minutes."

It was well past midnight so I called a cab to get me to the station. Sullivan met me outside and took me through the garage entrance directly to the basement. We walked past a row of empty holding cells into a brightly lit room at the end. It looked like a small gym—weights, treadmill, sauna, hydrotherapy tub—and I turned to Sullivan, confused. Behind him, Amit Samejo slammed the heavy steel door shut.

"Look out!" I yelled, but Samejo made no move toward us. I felt a hand clap hard on my mouth, a long arm wrap over my chest. I caught a glimpse in a mirror of Detective Sullivan holding me.

I fought, but his grip was like iron. Crushing both arms against my ribs, twisting my neck back. I worked my jaw until I managed to sink my teeth into the skin under Sullivan's thumb, but he didn't react. At all.

I called to Edgar, all his perceptions attuned to my panic. I could feel the layout of the room, sense Sullivan's position behind me. There. His foot, right next to mine. I lifted my knee and brought the spike of my shoe heel down, dead on his toe. I hit the concrete floor; he'd shifted just enough to avoid my stomp. I worked an arm free, tried to elbow his ribs. He caught my wrist and pulled, spilling me to the floor. I landed into a canvas—through Edgar's eyes, I'd seen Samejo sprawl it out. It was folded over me and bound with nylon straps.

I was gripped by the ankles and shoulders, Edgar watching as Sullivan and Samejo hoisted me like a board and carried me to the large, steel tub. It was full of ice and water. I felt the shock as I broke the surface, the overflow rushing out as they pushed me under. Someone put a heavy weight disc over my face and it pinned me to the bottom.

In freezing water. Crushed by blackness. Every primal fear, every night terror I had as a child, collapsed in on me. One chance.

Edgar, help me.

I saw more clearly through Edgar's vision than I ever had before. Sullivan and Samejo standing over the tub where I was drowning, holding me down. I told Edgar to attack them, to invade their bodies and their thoughts. As violently as possible.

Just one instant of distraction, a moment with their hands off me, and I would be able to push up... take a breath... fight ... survive.

Edgar. I'm dying. Save me.

And in that moment, I felt him abandon me.

The intimacy I'd known for twenty years, in every part of my body, in the shape my mind took every waking moment, ripped away. Edgar left me, lifting away like a balloon released by a child, as I smothered in the freezing blackness.

This is how I end. In agony and despair. Defeated. Violated. Alone.

I surrender to my death.

"She's coming around."

I see light. Clean fluorescent light. White walls. White ceiling tiles. A white sheet over my body. I can breathe.

I gasp air. Cool, nourishing air.

I look around. I am in a bed. A hospital room. There's a doctor in scrubs looking at a machine connected to my arm. I can't move. My wrists and ankles are bound by straps, not tight, but unyielding. Amit Samejo is at the foot of my bed. Detective Sullivan by the side.

"Bastards!" I scream. I thrash. I spit at them, but my mouth is so dry nothing comes out.

Then I feel it. Emptiness. No presence. No Edgar.

I sob like a child. I can't help it.

"I'm sorry," I hear Sullivan say. There is genuine pain in his voice. His eyes are misting. Samejo is openly weeping.

"It was the only way," he continues.

"What did you do to me?"

"We had to separate you. It had to be real. Your fear. You had to believe you were going to die. It's the only thing that will make them leave. I'm sorry. I truly am."

"He's gone," I say. "Edgar's gone."

"Yes," says Samejo, still weeping. "You're free."

"Why?" I demand. "Why did you do this to me? Who gave you the right?!"

Sullivan leans close to me. "These beings. Familiars. They don't belong in our world. They're broken, twisted—the most petty and spiteful of their kind—and they look for cracks in our reality, for the most vulnerable people to enter. To feed off. You didn't share a bond. You were kidnapped. Nidra Samejo realized the truth of it, realized what needed to be done. She came to me months ago and helped me understand. I'm going to show you what she showed me, because we need you to understand."

He takes a step forward and I feel a rush enter me.

The room's cold light blossoms and the bare walls dissolve. Without moving, I am transported, shifting from the solid place I inhabit to an ethereal elsewhere. I can see it. With my waking eyes I can see that other world, invisibly interlaced with ours. I see Edgar's world.

Before me is a figure—a being like Edgar—but vast and beautiful, radiating wisdom and compassion. There is no word to describe what I behold other than "goddess." Surrounding her are others like her, lesser, but no less magnificent. But there are also smaller creatures, bent and twisted, sullen and selfish. I recognize Edgar among them.

The goddess speaks my name.

They are my children, she says without words or sound but pure clarity. *Some hide from me and cling to you, unconcerned with the harm they cause. Forgive them. They know no better.*

The truth, flooding into me from this mother-goddess, is undeniable. Familiars, her wayward children, are sad, perverse things addicted to sensations of flesh they lack. I know it now. It shames me to realize I have always known it.

I come to collect them. Help me, Martine. Help me bring them home.

The connection ends, and I am once more in the plain hospital room. I start sobbing again, this time for completely different reasons.

I look to Samejo. "Your sister?"

"She trusted me," he gasps, tears streaming down his face. "She begged me to help her. I tried. I… let her… I let her fall. Oh, god! I let her fall."

He all but collapses. Sullivan places a hand on his shoulder.

"I should have been there," he says. "I'm sorry, my friend. It's my fault."

Detective Sullivan loosens the straps and helps me sit up in bed. I want to hit him. I want to ball up my fists and pound my rage on his lanky body, his impassive face. But I just lean into him and cry.

He holds me in his arms and strokes my back. The way my father used to, before Edgar entered my body, and he lost the will to even look me in the eye without disgust.

"What do I do now?" I ask.

"You help us find and free people afflicted by these parasites," he says. "There are others, like you, that have been released. You can lead them, Martine. Lead them the way Nidra Samejo wanted to before… before... we failed her."

I lean back, look up at Sullivan. I am wretched. Injured. But I feel myself—only myself—as I have not since childhood. It is like a raw open wound. But it is mine. Mine and mine alone. A pain of pure clarity.

"How do we begin?" I ask.

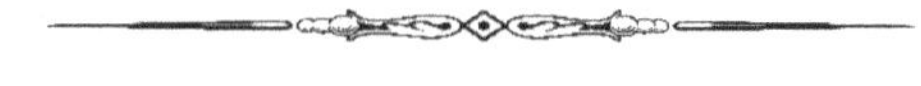

Matt McHugh was born in suburban Pennsylvania, attended LaSalle University in Philadelphia, and after a few years as a Manhattanite, currently calls New Jersey home. Website: mattmchugh.com

The Leisure Class

M. Luke McDonell

The jani-bots that kept Santa Monica's public streets spotlessly clean didn't venture down the private alleys. Joe picked his way carefully down the narrow, canyon-like space, side-stepping spent meth chargers, giving the reeking dumpsters wide berth, and dodging black puddles of god-knew-what. It hadn't rained in Los Angeles in months.

La Enoteca, midway down the block, was an isle of clean in the sea of filth. Joe had taken charge of the area behind the restaurant, scrubbing the asphalt with a push broom and bleach, and painting over the tweaker's crude graffiti with sky blue paint—not because it was part of his job but because he was proud of where he worked.

He nudged open the squeaky screen door and joined the cacophony of the kitchen. Dinner prep was in full swing, the high-ceilinged room almost geologically active with steam and fire. He danced around Francesca and her tray of perfect gnocchi, turned the corner to his station— and stopped dead. A four-armed silver cylinder the height of two garbage cans stood in his spot in front of the double sinks, plucking dirty plates from the pile,

rinsing them, and loading them into the small sanitizing dishwasher—all at once. The arms were triple- or quadruple-jointed, moving jerkily and way too fast. Joe watched, horrified, as the thing flew through the pile of lunch dishes. Someone had already tied an apron around its midsection.

He jumped when his manager slapped him on the back.

"Congratulations! You've been automated! You'll still get paid, you just don't have to come to work."

Anton, the sous chef, minced garlic and glared.

"I don't understand," said Joe.

"Come to my office."

As Joe made his way through the kitchen, his friends and coworkers watched him with expressions ranging from pity to resentment. Clarissa, a career waitress with bleached blond hair and a foul mouth, wrapped him in a hug.

"We'll miss you. I don't like Robby. The robot," she clarified when Joe looked puzzled.

Eduardo, a busboy, shook his head. "How'd you get this sweet deal, man? Money for nothing? It's bullshit.

Automate me," he challenged the manager.

"No metallic front-of-house staff in my restaurant," the manager declared, grinning.

The office, a closet of a room, stank of burnt oil and last night's tuna. Joe sat on a folding chair, numbly signing forms and trying to concentrate on his manager's words. Health benefits, counseling, education vouchers. None of this made any sense. In the background he heard rhythmic, metallic clanging and the chime of clean plates being stacked.

Sure, he'd complained about his job. Sore feet. Aching back. But he liked working here. He fed off the energy and camaraderie. The slowly rising tempo as the sun set, golden light sneaking through the screen door and creeping across the concrete floor. The Prosecco glasses and small plates of happy hour giving way to big, greasy bowls smeared with house-made pasta sauce and drained-dry carafes of house red and oily pizza pans. The winding down after the last seating, grabbing a quick bite of *gnocchi al ragu* before tackling the big pots, burned saucepans, and the cast iron frying pans he wasn't allowed to put in the dishwasher. The busboys filing out the back, each of them wishing him a good night as he shoved the last load of plates into the sanitizer. It was a good place to work with good people.

"I've sent a paycheck to your account for the last eight days; the government will take it from here." The manager slicked back his already slick black hair and consulted his laptop. "It may take up to a month for you to receive your first payment from them, but after that you'll be paid every two weeks."

He held out his hand, palm up. "I'll need your uniform."

Joe glanced at the duffle bag. "I forgot it. I was going to borrow one from Giovanni."

The manager's smile held, thin and chill. "Ah. Well. Drop it off when you have a chance."

"I will."

The manager collected pages from the copy machine and handed the disordered stack to Joe. "You're part of the new leisure class. Enjoy yourself."

Joe's wife, Emilia, was skeptical, then enthused. "You can take the kids to school *and* pick them up! We won't need childcare anymore. We can all have dinner together and you can cook!"

Emilia, a receptionist at a Century 21 real estate office, worked normal business hours Monday through Friday, whereas Joe had worked Tuesday through Saturday 4p.m. to midnight.

She did some rapid calculations. "We're coming out ahead, babe, even if you only get a 2% raise a year." She pulled him close, kissed him. "You can work on your comics. You're such a good artist. I wanna find out what happens to, what's his name? Artemis? You left off right in the middle of the series."

Joe hadn't drawn with anything but crayons since Timothy was born, and little of that after Clementine, thanks to her colic. He wasn't sure he remembered how to use a stylus and the animation software he liked had gone through so many upgrades in the last eight years he probably wouldn't know how to use it.

Joe attended the mandatory counseling session, held in a repurposed Department of Motor Vehicles building. No need for it now that all the cars were city-owned and driverless, yet the crowds and disorganization felt all too familiar. He took a number and sat on a dirty plastic bench beside a woman in her mid-50s who chatted on her phone in Cantonese.

He hadn't realized so many people had been displaced by robots. His restaurant boasted an all-human staff and he'd been sure his job was safe.

When his number was finally called and he moved from one plastic seat to another, it was clear that his counselor, Maryann, had been in hers far too long. She pushed unwashed brown bangs from a forehead dashed by stress acne.

"Joe Sicilia. Congratulations on your promotion. You are now free to pursue your dreams. You can attend any community college at no charge. Public transportation within the city of Los Angeles is free with this voucher. Here is a list of meet-ups where you can find like-minded people and pursue common goals. Do you have any questions?"

He didn't. He went home and tried to draw. He failed, the pressure of the hours of free time driving the stylus too hard onto the tablet and ruining the lines.

Emilia, and many others, began to wear their uniforms when they didn't need to. His next-door neighbor, Sandra, worked the evening shift at the Santa Monica Hilton, but when she climbed on the bus in the morning with her kids, she was already dressed in black and gray polyester, shiny plastic nametag on her breast.

After while she stopped greeting Joe, making do with a barely perceptible nod as she hustled her kids to the back of the bus where the other uniformed parents congregated. Joe examined his jeans and Hawaiian shirt. He looked much better now than he had when he worked at La Enoteca…didn't he?

After he got the kids to school, he went home and retrieved his duffle bag from a dusty shelf in the garage. The white shirt, embroidered with his first name, smelled faintly of citrus and garlic. He washed it—and the hound's-tooth pants. Why the manager made them wear those ridiculous pants he'd never know, but he put them on now, struggling with the zipper—he'd gained a few pounds. The shirt still fit fine.

He walked to the corner and waited for the bus. When it arrived, he hoisted himself up the stairs and manoeuvred through the crush to the back to join the others in uniform. He nodded. They nodded back.

When they returned to looking out the windows or playing with screens, he pulled out a sketchbook and tried to capture their expressions with pencil and paper. He wasn't drawing, not really, just capturing the moment. Maybe that should be someone's job. The robots certainly weren't doing it. When the woman he was sketching grinned, the tentative gray line shot up and to the right. Joe couldn't help smiling as well. He'd gotten it.

The bus headed south on the Pacific Coast Highway. Joe doodled a pair of loose linen pants, a bioactive t-shirt that would change patterns based on mood, a fez with a display screen, and sandals with soles thick enough to handle the hazards of city streets. The uniform of a 21st century artist—if he could get Emilia to create it for him. She'd always wanted to be a fashion designer. Her sewing machine languished in the garage, sharing a shelf with the earthquake supplies. He'd get it cleaned up and working so that when she walked into the real estate office and found a robot slouched behind her desk, she wouldn't have to join the leisure class either.

He contemplated the nub of a pencil, badly in need of sharpening and eraser nearly gone. Maybe he should switch to colored pastels. He'd need color for the future he was imagining. Emilia's grin would definitely be bright red.

M. Luke McDonell's five-minutes-into-the-future fiction explores the effects of emerging technology on individuals and society. Her work has appeared in Shoreline of Infinity, The Overcast, The Arcanist, Perihelion, New Reader Magazine, and more. Additionally, she produces the SF in SF podcast, a monthly author reading event.

By day, she is a senior visual designer by night she writes and helps run SomaFM internet radio. Follow her on Twitter @Mlukemc and learn more at /mlukemcdonell.wordpress.com

End Times

Brian Maycock

There are dead men in the street laughing in the rain and not an umbrella in sight. Smoke climbs into the sky as sirens rise and fall. Silence has replaced the soundtrack of TV soaps that used to seep through constantly from the semi next door. There's nothing on anyway since the emergency broadcast went dark. My wife is slumped on the sofa groaning, asking for brains. Her skin has begun to fall away, and it turns out she's not beautiful inside, no matter how many bake stalls she ran for charity before the apocalypse made zombies of us all.

Brian Maycock lives in Glasgow and is currently writing a novel.

Miser

Thomas J. Griffin

On the Proving Grounds there are only winners and dead men. It's not just about winning for me, though. I was so close, just two matches left...

When you fall short, the Aurelia Syndicates don't give second chances. They throw you in the incinerator, then wipe your name from the ledger. I'm left to die in a room called the Hurt Locker. It's a waystation between the arena and the morgue, a stripped O.R. with floor-to-ceiling porcelain tile and a drain at its center where the losers are left to bleed out. I've already lost so much blood by the time they drag me in, it takes a good two minutes for me to notice the others present. Dark suits, darker looks-- Syndicate, not doctors, but why they're here to watch me die is beyond whatever faculties I have left. The Syndicates don't give second chances, do they?

There are two of them, a severe-looking woman in a heavy black peacoat and her muscle, his collar left unbuttoned around a too-thick neck. They regard me from a safe distance, the woman appraising, the muscle wary, as if I could do any more than cough blood on them at this point. My left arm is gone at the elbow, taken off by a gravity axe, my right eye smashed from the socket. He'd been called Atlas, the bastard who got me, and he'd looked like the statues, let me tell you. Near seven feet tall and cut from marble. Hardly bothered to wear clothes, let alone armor. That axe was all he'd needed, impossibly big and glowing like a stove coil. Still, I'd thought I could take him.

I'd been wrong.

"Don't look so great," the severe woman says to me. Even for a crime boss, she's good at deadpan.

"I'll shake it off."

"We could help with that."

"Didn't think the Syndicates..." I start, but somewhere along the way those last few words get lost in the fog. It feels like someone is going from room to room, turning off the lights of my mind and pulling the doors closed behind them.

The woman shakes her head knowingly. "We don't."

"Then… why?" My tongue is going slowly numb, as is the rest of me. I lie back on the examination table, saving my breath. Somehow, I'm able to keep my one good eye focused. It sees the woman step closer, her stilettos tracking right through a pool of blood. My blood.

"Because we need a dead man."

"How dead?"

"Awfully glib, for someone in your position."

"Not a lot… left to lose."

"So you say, but we know why you entered the Proving Grounds," says the woman. She cracks a smile, slight but full of menace. "Help us and we won't only save you."

Some people say you see a white light before you die. Others claim your life flashes before your eyes. For me, though, the death throes bring a simple clarity. The Syndicate woman is right. I'm here for a purpose, and if I can't fulfill it in life, maybe I can in death.

"Where do I sign?"

I wake up in a hospital room. A real one, with soft linen bedsheets and privacy curtains and windows to let in natural sunlight. Arrayed around my bed is a fleet of expensive-looking machinery, every device beeping and blinking independently, but all in some way connected to me. To my left, a heartrate monitor chirps steadily, more or less, and the rhythm is oddly calming. The last thing I remember with any sort of lucidity is being certain I was about to die; the monitor's bleep is a simple testimony to the contrary, but it is powerful nonetheless. I hadn't wanted to die, but I also hadn't thought I had a choice.

I flex a big toe experimentally. Ouch. Stiff, but alive. It's not until I try flexing everything else that I realize I have everything else, namely my left arm. I can feel it hiding under the bedsheet, each digit accounted for. It isn't even sore. Slowly, half afraid it's a phantom sensation, I withdraw my hand from under the sheet.

Not my hand. At least, not my old one.

My screams crackle like static, my throat raw from disuse. The sound doesn't bounce or echo, but sinks into the walls, leaving behind a concussive quiet. No doctors come rushing in, no concerned nurses or orderlies. No one even pokes their head through the door to check if I'm all right. Despite my panic I find this strange--what kind of hospital leaves a patient in critical care unattended, out of earshot?

"I think he's awake," a voice mumbles from beyond the privacy curtain.

"No shit, Toro."

The curtain to my left slides back. Behind it stand my new friends, the severe woman and her muscle--Toro, I presume. They stare frankly, waiting for me to catch my breath.

"What… the hell," I say, my voice still hoarse.

"A strange way to say thank you."

"You did this to me?" I hold up my arm, now matte grey and ribbed like a braided steel cord. The back of the hand, I notice for the first time, is inset with a glass bulb, like the kind that blinks once the oven has pre-heated. I can barely look at it.

"We own your contract. We can do whatever we want to you… with your consent."

"But why?" I ask, watching my new fingers twitch out of the corner of my eye.

The severe woman looks bemused. "Don't you remember? We need a dead man, not a half of one."

I finally recall the death bed deal I made. I don't remember actually signing anything, but clearly that hasn't stopped the Hunt Brothers, the syndicate that owns my contract, from turning me into a cyborg.

"You haven't even noticed the eye yet, have you?"

"The..." I'd forgotten. My right eye had been smashed by that brute, Atlas. With my good hand--my old hand--I reach up and touch the flesh surrounding it, but everything feels normal.

"Look at me and wink," the severe woman commands. I do, and a neon orange reticle pops into view over her face. I wink several more times, watching the target flash on and off. Then I look at Toro, but the reticle stays on the woman, glowing brightly in my periphery.

"Handy, right?" she asks. "Toro here swears by it."

The muscle is wearing dark sunglasses, and as he tips them forward, I catch a flash like a laser pointer. I recoil, unnerved by the inhumanness of it. Toro shoots me a cinderblock smile.

"Top of the line for security personnel," The severe woman continues. "It's also got built-in infrared. And try this. Raise your hand and squeeze your fist tight."

The metallic hand is already moving, nearly independent of my will. Deliberately, cautiously, I curl each finger into a fist, and as my thumb wraps overtop of the knuckles, there's a faint click. The inset bulb flashes crimson and my arm straightens, pointing directly at the severe woman, who can't seem to contain her glee.

"It's a *pulse fist,* and it's synced with the targeting system in your eye. The latest bionics, hellishly expensive. All you have to do is twist your wrist palm-down while it's locked on, and you'll fire off an electrical charge big enough to drop a rhino."

I've been fighting back alarm this whole time, but at her words a wild thought sneaks through the anxiety. I keep my arm steady, staring at the woman until her expression sours.

"Put it down," she says dismissively, but behind the anger I can also hear the high notes of fear. I keep my fist raised until Toro steps between us, huffing like a bull moose.

I drop my arm at last, giving my fingers another experimental stretch. For the first time in a long time I feel some measure of control, and it goes a long way toward calming me. I look on the severe woman and her muscle with a new confidence.

"So the Hunt Brothers have made me into their weapon. Why?"

"I told you at the Proving Grounds," the woman says, impatient. I've flustered her. "We need a dead man for a job, and you fit the bill. You were dead a month, long enough for your death to be registered officially with the county, and all your I.D. beacons removed."

"But why me specifically?" I ask. "Why not kill one of your members and bring them back off the grid?"

The severe woman pushes Toro away and slides closer to my bedside, showing me she's no longer scared. "Frankly? Because it's not that easy to kill someone. At least, not legally. And you're a good fighter, the best we have under a gladiatorial contract. Or, you were..."

"So you need somebody tough killed, and you don't want it traced back to you afterward."

The severe woman's wicked smile returns. "You're finally getting it."

"Who's the target?"

A moment's hesitation as her smile again fades. "Miser."

The bleep to my left quickens noticeably. The severe woman marks it, but doesn't tease. She understands. Miser is the leader of Aurelia City's strongest syndicate, Iron Tribe, and he has a reputation for over-the-top ruthlessness, even among those who make a living being ruthless.

"How?" I ask, all my confidence shattered. "I've never even seen him before."

The severe woman shrugs. "No one has, not outside the Tribe, but that's your problem." Toro chuckles, and she motions for him to get the door. "You're being discharged this afternoon. You have another month. If you do manage to kill him, we'll pay out your contract in full. If you can't... well, do us a favor and die quick, without giving us up. I don't think I need to tell you how the Hunt Brothers handle betrayal, even from beyond the vale. Just because you're dead, doesn't mean we can't hurt you. Savvy?"

I nod, my tongue gone dry, and the severe woman leaves without another word. Once again I'm alone with the beeping machines. I suppose I'm one of them now.

East Aurelia is a tough neighborhood, grown harder with age, like the trunk of an old oak tree. Nothing changes here; new businesses won't move in because they don't want to pay into the Iron Tribe racket, and those that are already established will never have to close up, the corner shops getting to keep their corners so long as they pay the protection costs. And why wouldn't they? There is no petty crime in East Aurelia. Like any mob worth its reputation, the Iron Tribe has monopolized felony on the east side of town, civilized it, keeping the streets cleaner than the police ever cared to, even before they stopped caring. An irony, certainly, but most in East Aurelia don't see it that way. To them, the only difference between the police and the Syndicates is that one answers their calls.

It's no simple thing to walk around this neighborhood a stranger. It's nothing like the downtown loop, with surveillance cams on every block to track your gait and scan your retinas, but that doesn't mean there isn't security to circumvent. East Aurelia is old-school. Everybody knows everybody, and nobody's looking to talk, not even to give directions. It takes me a week to find the Iron Tribe headquarters, and another to find a rooftop I can spy from without drawing the attention of their spotters. My new eye has already come in handy on that account--not only can the night vision identify and record individual heat signatures, it has a zoom feature. This means I can watch safely from three blocks away and six stories up, at night, until I find who I'm looking for.

He's a courier, always coming and going, always through one of the side doors. Most everyone who leaves Iron Tribe HQ employs the buddy system, but not this guy, making him the perfect mark. After a few days I start following him on his runs, which almost always take him downtown, to a particular high rise off Broadway and 12th Avenue. I track him all the way to the penthouse. This is my guy.

The next time I see him leaving headquarters, I make my move. I know all his routes by heart and catch him down an alley before he can get to his ride. I let him pass, then step out behind and grab him by the collar.

"What the-" the courier starts, then cuts himself short when he feels the muzzle of my gun press into the small of his back. It's unloaded, but he doesn't need to know that.

"No sudden moves, no loud noises," I say quietly. "I don't want to hurt you, but I will."

The courier twitches under my grip, but stays put. With his line of work, this is doubtless not the first time he's been held at gunpoint. Don't shoot the messenger is one of history's great ignored maxims.

"Who is Miser?"

"You serious?" The courier shifts, trying to sneak a peek of me over his shoulder, so I jerk him around a bit. "Okay okay, jeez. Nobody knows who Miser is. Everyone knows that."

"Fine, where can I find him then?"

"How should I know? I'm just a thrall."

"Oh yeah? And if I go to that penthouse on Twelfth, I won't find him there?"

His breath catches. He hesitates for a second, then whispers, "If I tell you anything, they'll kill me." I'd have to be deaf not to hear his fear, and momentarily I'm torn. I don't want to be here. I don't want to do this, but I have to.

"If you don't tell me what I want to know, I'll kill you right now."

The courier tenses again, but keeps his mouth shut. A real veteran, this one. Maybe I picked wrong. I've only got a week left to finish the job, yet I'm no closer to my target. I need answers quickly, and if this guy can't give me what I need, I'll have to get rid of him fast and reset.

Or... maybe not.

"You said you're a thrall. How much do you owe the Tribe?"

The alley around us is perfectly quiet, so when the courier sighs, it fills the space like a foghorn. "I'll be Iron Tribe the rest of my life," he says flatly. It's not indifference. It's resignation. A thrall is what the Syndicates call their debtors, slaves in all but name, men and women who have entered into a long-term contract with the Syndicates in exchange for assistance, be it financial, medical, legal, or criminal. The terms of these contracts are rarely generous, typically no less than five years of labor, but then, they can be as harsh as they want. They're designed for the desperate. If this guy's in for life, he must owe a fortune.

"What if you weren't? I could help you." I spin him around so he can see my face, and I his. He's the definition of nondescript--white, soft face, weak chin, hair dark brown and receding above the temples. Early to mid-forties. He doesn't smile, but he's not hostile, either, though he does glance repeatedly at my right eye. I know from the few times I've checked a mirror that it has a faint, opalescent gleam, but instead of hiding it, I stare back, quashing my self-conscious impulses. This is what I am now.

"I'm a thrall, just like you, but I've been given a second chance. If I can get to Miser, my employer will square my debt. Help me, and they'll square yours too." It's a lie, but I'd rather use this guy than kill him.

"The Syndicates don't give second chances," the courier says by rote. I don't need the enhanced perception of my new eye to read the doubt on his face.

"They did for me, and they could for you too. Think about it. You could stop being their fetch-and-carry. You could be free."

It's that last word that hooks him. Free. He takes it in like a breath of pure O_2, holding it, letting it fill him up. He's still scared--of me, of the Syndicates--but there's conflict there now. Not many of us get a second crack at freedom once we've signed it away.

"What would I have to do?" the courier asks, but with an odd gleam in his eye. He's already in, even if he hasn't realized it yet.

I tap a finger next to my bionic eye. The thump sprays static across my vision. "Just show me the way in."

"So what should I call you, partner?"

We sit in a VR café on the west side of town, outside of Iron Tribe territory. It wouldn't do to be overheard by some Tribe snitch grabbing lunch on his way to work. We've taken a booth in the front room and ordered coffees, which arrive by serving drone only moments later. There are no human servers, except for a single attendant paid to sit in the corner and look bored until one of the order screens malfunctions or somebody wants their money back. Every few minutes, someone stumbles out of the back room, where they keep the VR pods, and sits down in the nearest open booth, looking clammy and unstable. Good VR will do that to you. It's like a drug, a full body rush, and coming out leaves you disoriented and fatigued, like being woken up during REM sleep. Whoever decided to pair it with a coffee shop was an entrepreneurial genius. That said, I'm not a fan, myself. Tried it once and threw up in the pod halfway through.

The courier scans the mostly empty café before returning his focus to his coffee. He holds his mug in both hands, but doesn't sip, simply stares at it, watching the steam rise.

"Fauks."

"Like the animal?"

"Spelled different." The table is a touch screen, and he traces his name across it with a finger. This prompts an animation of a face to appear.

"YOUR REQUEST DOES NOT MATCH ANY OF THE ITEMS ON OUR MENU. HERE IS A LIST OF POPULAR ALTERNATIVES."

The café's menu blooms onscreen underneath our mugs. We ignore it.

"Well nice to meet you, Fauks," I say, and take a sip of my coffee. "I'm…" I stop, unsure how much I should tell my new friend. This Fauks may have decided to hear me out, but that doesn't mean I trust him.

He's watching me sidelong, waiting. He's got a natural shiftiness about him, this Fauks. Always staring out through his eyebrows at a suspicious world.

"Do you think you're still you, after you die?" I ask.

Fauks looks confused, and rightly so. "I'm not sure I know what you mean."

I grimace. "Long story short? I should be dead. I'm only back because I have a job to do."

"Yes, about that." It's Fauks's turn to grimace. "You know this is a suicide mission, right? Whether or not I help you, there's no chance you'll get away with killing Miser, even if you actually find him. This only ends with you dying."

"Then I guess it's a good thing I'm already dead," I say, but my joke falls flat. Fauks just looks sorry for me, like there's something about my own joke I don't get.

"Why are you even doing this?" For the first time since the alley, Fauks looks me in the eye. His stare is intense, laser focused, and it makes me feel as though I might not be the only one with superhuman vision. "It's not for you, is it."

Smart, for a courier thrall.

"No," I say, more than a little begrudgingly.

"A relative?" he asks. He looks genuinely concerned. "A parent, spouse?"

"A daughter."

"Sick?"

I nod. "She's got a rare blood disorder. It's taken a toll. She was on a transplant list, but..."

"But it was taking too long," Fauks says with all the understanding of someone who has spent too many hours in the waiting room of a federal urgent care clinic. We all have, at one point or another. "Still, why turn to the Syndicates?"

"Had to, especially after I got caught trying to bribe our physician. I didn't have a choice, the line was too long. She was going to die on it! But now she's been pulled from the list entirely and it's all because of me, because of what I did and..." I suck on my tongue to keep my lip from quivering. "The Syndicates understand that sometimes the law only gets in the way. They've got their own doctors who aren't bound by all the regulation and bureaucracy. And they do amazing work." I raise my left hand as evidence. "All I had to do was win the grand prize at the Proving Grounds. The Hunt Brothers get the winnings, and my daughter gets the treatment she needs."

"But if you're here..."

"Yep." I smile ruefully, feeling stupid. Only two more wins.

"That explains how you died." Fauks's grin fades when I don't return it, and we sit there for a minute in hesitant silence.

"So... your route. Who lives in that penthouse? Is it Miser?"

Fauks shakes his head. "No, it belongs to his number two, a man named Boyle. He manages the day-to-day for Iron Tribe, and I bring him zip files of the stuff they only keep on local servers, off the official books."

For some reason I find it amusing that a syndicate would even have *official* books. Appearances, I suppose. "You make your deliveries to Boyle directly?"

"God no, I barely get past the front door. I trade off with one of his thugs, then head back to HQ." He finally takes a sip of his coffee and makes a restrained *I don't like coffee* face. "But what's it matter? Boyle isn't the guy you want anyway."

"Not necessarily," I say. "If there's one person in the Tribe who could actually lead me to Miser, it's his right-hand man, don't you think?"

Fauks nods his head slowly, his eyes flashing back and forth across the table. The gears are turning now. "You know, there have been rumors for months of trouble between Boyle and Miser. Why not test his loyalty? Might be, he's willing to help you along."

This is exactly what I want to hear. Whoever Miser is, he's hidden himself well, but no man is an island. Boyle could be my ticket, if I can get to him. "If you don't have direct access to Boyle, who does?"

Fauks absently picks up his mug, then sets it back down. "Your best bet would be one of his security detail, I think. One of the thugs who guard his doors."

"I'd rather not fight anyone." I say, frowning. Couriers are one thing, but it will be hard to get the drop on a trained guard.

"Weren't you a Proving Grounds gladiator?"

"Yes... but that doesn't mean I like hurting people."

Fauks scowls at me, nonplussed.

I sigh. "Got any specific targets in mind?"

He sits back and scratches his chin, looking stumped. Then the back door slams open, and a man comes stumbling out. He's a clear case of bad VR trip, his suit, a tan two-piece, soaked through at the pits, his tie jerked loose. Flushed and unsteady, he collapses into the first booth on the right and begins swiping hurriedly across the tabletop, invariably ordering something strong and black. His finger leaves a Kandinsky-esque trail of sweat splotches across the surface.

Fauks's face lights up. "Actually, I think I know just the guy. His name is Atlas."

That name. My left arm twitches, the hand clinching, activating the pulse fist involuntarily.

Maybe I wouldn't mind a fight after all.

Even tilted drunk, Atlas sees me coming and manages to dodge the first swing. Probably he marked me back in the bar, recognized my face from the Proving Grounds. That would explain his look now, like he's seen a ghost. After all, he thinks he killed me months ago. Perhaps I'm not the first dead man who's come back to haunt him.

The arena for our rematch is a subway tunnel, an interstitial link in the underground maze between lines. At this time of night the tunnel is functionally abandoned, the rush of foot traffic ebbing hours ago. It's half-lit, only one bulb in three glowing a wan yellow, barely enough to differentiate individual floor stains from their cement canvas.

"Y-you." He staggers back, catching himself on the railing, and points at me with a meaty finger. "You... I... it's impossible."

"Is it?" I ask, grinning. I can only imagine what I look like to him, face scarred not quite beyond recognition, my

bionic eye watching with unblinking focus, iridescent despite the low light. This thing is a marvel, tracking Atlas's every twitch under the reticle, measuring his heightened pulse, analyzing posture. His right arm is highlighted by a faint, red overlay, a looping hook the most probable attack based on stance and muscle tension.

He sets his feet wider to steady himself, compensating for what is likely a considerable liquor drunk, according to the eye's analysis of his movements. Atlas is a fighter though, and a good one, dangerous no matter his condition, so I ready myself. There's an almost subaudible buzz as the pulse fist activates.

Atlas takes a first, brave step off the wall of the tunnel. He's already overcoming that initial fear, testing me. "What are you?"

"Come and see."

My eye reads his punch instantly. He's still deadly quick, especially for a brute his size, but I manage to duck and come back with my own haymaker. The charged pulse fist lands to his rib cage with a flash that lights the tunnel. There's a sizzle like a bug zapper scorching a fly, and Atlas goes down, his knees buckling from the shock.

The fight's over before it even begins, and briefly I'm ashamed. I'd wanted my moment of revenge to last longer. This was my would-be killer. He'd taken my arm, my eye, and my life without so much as a thought, yet defeating him so easily somehow makes me feel even weaker by comparison. But then, I'm not me, anymore. Not really. Bionics are banned in the Proving Grounds. For good reason, apparently.

Electrical tremors still course through Atlas, but he's no quitter. Weakly he tries to press himself up off the floor, so I bring my boot across his jaw. It drops him, this time for good.

"Is it done?" Fauks peeks out from his hiding spot around the corner. Seeing the prone Atlas, he braves the turn and joins me in the tunnel.

"Dead?"

"No, just unconscious."

Fauks takes a quick step back. "Well hurry up and finish it then. Who knows when somebody will come this way."

I give Fauks an incredulous look. "I'm not going to kill him. You said we only need his thumbprint, right?"

"The whole thumb would be better." He hits me with an iron stare, the kind which makes me question my own fortitude. I'd not thought this unassuming man capable of such hardness. "Why show him mercy? Did he show you any the last time?"

I don't say anything out loud; there's no need. My body is the evidence. Still, when Atlas cut me down, at least I was standing. To slay the defenseless is something altogether different, and the idea of it further sours the taste of my revenge.

"This man tried to kill you. He came between you and your daughter. What are you going to do about it?"

I look at Fauks, returning his hard stare with interest. "I was hired to kill one man only, and that's what I'm going to do. We can take the thumb without taking his life."

The tunnel lights flicker, dipping Fauks in and out of shadow as he regards me. The moment stretches taut, but he finally concedes with a shrug.

"All right then, do it your way." He reaches into his pocket, then holds his hand out to me. On his palm rests a switchblade.

I take it.

I lean forward out of the stairwell, trying and failing to look inconspicuous. The corridor is blessedly empty, though I can hear voices in conversation around the corner. It's an ICU, so someone is never far away, but all I want is a moment.

At the end of the corridor is a private room. I steal toward it as quietly as I can, keeping my eyes low, my hands in my pockets. The door is unlocked, but I don't dare enter, instead hovering just outside, staring in through the large double-paned window which faces into the hall.

My daughter is asleep, which relieves me, as being awake often means being in pain for her. It also means she can't see me, won't know I was here. I keep my right eye closed, not wanting whatever readout of her status it would give me. It's hard enough to look with plain sight. She's hooked up to a variety of monitors and drips, just like I was, but unlike me, she's not getting fixed; she's getting worse. The doctors can keep her floating, but dialysis only puts off the inevitable. Her chart hangs from a hook by the door, and all it takes is a glance to confirm what I already know. Words like "End Stage" never get easier to read. I focus on the top of the chart instead, on her name.

<u>Lilly Ottman</u>

It makes me smile despite myself. I've always thought it a pretty name, the only thing I've ever given her that didn't turn out wrong.

"Excuse me, sir? Are you allowed to be up here?"

I'm no longer alone. A man advances on me from the opposite end of the corridor, an orderly or male nurse judging by his powder blue scrubs. I open my right eye reflexively and the reticle latches onto him, a burning orange target over the center of his chest.

"Sir, who are you? I'm going to need to see some I.D. This is a closed ward."

I scrunch my eyes closed to clear the display, then steal one last glance through Lilly's window. She's still resting, peacefully. A good image to take with me as I go, ducking around the corner and fleeing down a second stairwell. This isn't the first time I've done this, but hopefully it will be the last.

Fauks greets me with a nod by the back door. He's already called a car, which idles, driverless, by the curb. Silently we climb in, and I punch our next address into the touchpad interface.

Broadway and 12th Avenue, Aurelia City.

The most stressful elevator ride of my life is quietly undercut by the sounds of smooth jazz playing from a speaker in the ceiling. A soft *ding*, not quite in time with the elevator music, marks the passing of each floor. The arrhythmia only adds to my anxiety, as does the endless upward procession. Aurelia City began growing up long ago, when it could no longer grow out, and this upscale residential is one of its tallest. I've no great fear of heights, but certain altitudes would get to anyone. I keep my back to the window, my eyes on the double doors, and my focus on the jazz, telling myself that I only imagine the air getting thinner.

The final *ding* is a triple tone, indicating the end of the ride. Penthouse level. The elevator doors slide open, but I don't step out yet. I hold my finger against the button to keep them spread and look at my partner.

"Are you sure you want to come with me?" I whisper.

Fauks gives me a jerky nod. He looks a little flushed, but it seems excitement more than fear.

"I don't need you for this part."

"Maybe not, but on the off-chance you don't die, I want to be here to collect on the promise you made me."

"Fair enough," I say, then make to leave the elevator, but Fauks snatches me back.

"Forgetting something?"

"Oh, right." I bring my left hand in front of my face, studying it for a moment. Despite its steel grey contours and its unnatural weight, I'm already growing used to it. Already thinking of it as *my hand*. I curl it into a fist, squeezing until I hear the click, the low microwave hum of live current. "Okay, let's do it."

I burst from the elevator at a sprint, banking left. At the end of the hall, no more than twenty paces away, is a single door, double wide and opal black, like a beetle's shell. Next to it, hunched over a stool, is the guard Fauks warned me about. He startles at my approach, his expression going from glassy and half-lidded to wide-eyed alarm, but like Atlas he's a professional. His gun's out of his holster before he's even risen from his stool, but my bionic eye reads the motion in real-time, virtually marking the trajectory of the shot. I dodge at the last possible instant, the bullet coming so close I can feel the invisible concussion in my inner ear like a change in air pressure.

One shot is all the guard gets before my charged punch drives into his chest. It blasts him backward over his stool, toppling him head over heels. He lies crumpled in the corner of the hallway, insensate, his expression once again glassy.

Fauks steals up behind me while I'm still standing over the guard and taps me on the shoulder. When I look, he's holding out a plastic sandwich bag, the inside smeared with red.

A thought occurs to me as I reach for the bag, trying not to look directly at it. "Why did we need Atlas, if this guy was already stationed here? Can't he get us inside also?"

"Inside, yes," Fauks says, "but not into Boyle's study. That's why we needed Atlas. He's Boyle's chief of security. Complete access."

I almost drop the thumb, still slippery with blood as I remove it from the bag. I'd tried to clean it off after… relieving… it from Atlas's hand, but it must have bled more in transit. This won't do; it needs to be clean for the scanner. I work up some saliva, tasting bile in my mouth, and spit onto the dispossessed thumb, then rub it against my shirt until the print is clean and dry.

The scanner flashes green the moment the thumb touches, and the door pops open, revealing a darkling foyer. The lights above bloom automatically, leading the way deeper into the apartment, but I hesitate at the threshold, looking back at Fauks for reassurance.

"You go ahead. I'll keep a lookout here," he says, and prods the unconscious doorman with the toe of his boot. "Wouldn't want this one to wake back up while we're inside."

I glance at the fallen man and tell myself it was him or my Lilly. I would say the same thing after each fight in the Proving Grounds, to temper my resolve. I have to keep in mind why I'm doing this, or I won't be able to follow through. I look again to Fauks, who's been eyeing me with a curious expression.

"If I'm not back in ten minutes, go ahead and leave. No sense in us both getting caught."

He nods at that, so I leave him in the doorway. Then, just as I reach the end of the hall, his voice catches up with me.

"Check his office upstairs first. He usually works late."

The living room is quiet, empty. The automatic lights don't extend into the penthouse proper, but one wall is floor-to-ceiling windows, and the ambient glow from the city below is enough to light my path around the furniture, even without my night vision. I'm glad for that; I find seeing in infrared unsettling, spectral, the world an indistinct shimmer of colorblind heat.

Along the far wall of the living room is a spiral staircase. Ascending slowly, I emerge onto a second-level catwalk with doors at either end. One should be the office; the other likely a bedroom, but I can't tell which is which until I approach the door to my left and notice the print scanner embedded into the wood just above the knob. Once more I pluck Atlas's thumb from its zip lock home, dry it on my shirt, and press it to the scanner. Another flash of green, and the door opens on a lit study. A bookshelf covers the wall to my left, another floor-to-ceiling window opposite. A cherry desk dominates the center.

Standing behind the desk is a man. He's pointing a pistol at my head.

I dive into a roll, two bullets ripping into the door behind me. My tumble takes me right to the foot of the desk. I pop to my feet and lunge for the gun, but I'm too slow. A fraction before my hand closes around the muzzle, it flashes.

Smoke issues from between steel fingers. I can feel the bullet smashed against the center of my palm, but it didn't penetrate. It didn't even hurt. Closing my hand around the barrel, I wrench the gun away and toss it behind me.

"Mr. Boyle? I've got a couple questions for you."

If Boyle is stunned to see me survive his point-blank bullet, he doesn't show it. Instead he takes a swing for my head. My eye reads it instantly and I slip out of the way, returning a counter of my own, a right straight to the nose. It's with my normal hand, but it still does the trick. Dazed, Boyle collapses into his chair, and I hurry around his desk and take hold of him by the collar before he can gather his wits back.

"First question," I say, as though nothing's happened. "Who is Miser?"

"Who are you?" Boyle asks, a little slowly, but not without spite. He's groggy from my punch, but no sooner do his eyes clear than there's anger there. "Do you have any idea who you're messing with?"

"Do you?" I drag him up out of his seat so we're face to face, letting him get a good, long look into my right eye. I see a flicker of something pass over him, maybe fear, but to his credit, it's momentary. The anger snaps back into place, and instead of retorting he simply glowers at me.

He's stalling. In my periphery I mark a faint red light blinking away under his desk. An emergency signal, maybe for police, maybe for more goons like Atlas. Either way, I'm short on time. "Fine, second question. Where can I find Miser? Tonight."

"You won't find him at all. He'll find you first, and he'll kill you, just like he'll kill me if I tell you anything."

"And you think I won't?" Boyle's not scared of me, or at least, less so than he is of his boss. That needs to change, and fast. Holding him up with my right hand, I drag him to the window, charge the pulse fist, and touch it to the glass. The entire window shatters like it's been hit with a wrecking ball, shards exploding in every direction to stick in the carpet like caltrops.

Boyle's eyes are squeezed shut, and when he finally opens them, I see the whites. I hold him steady over the abyss, my fist an inch from his face, humming its microwave music. Lightning dances across my knuckles. The air between us smells like ozone.

"Okay, okay, just… God, watch where you wave that thing."

I push my fist closer, menacing, and a flash of static skips from my knuckle to Boyle's broken nose. He spasms, but lucky for him, I don't let him slip free.

"Dammit! You want to find Miser? Fine, it's actually not hard. You know our headquarters on the east side? He leaves there every day, same time, and comes h…"

Once again, I feel the bullet pass before I even hear the shot, and most of Boyle's head is gone faster than my eye can register. Not much faster, though; as his limp body slumps out of my grasp, I'm already turning, pulse fist raised like a shield to intercept the next shell. I'm out of time. The reinforcements Boyle called have arrived.

Except, they haven't. It's only Fauks. He holds Boyle's pistol in both hands, his eye still sighting down the barrel, following his shot, but as I watch he lowers it and smiles expectantly at me like a cat who's just brought home a dead bird to drop at my feet.

"What have you done?" I ask, stunned. "Why would you… he was just about to tell me who Miser is!"

"I know. You did well, much better than I thought you would." Fauks paces further into the room, circling to keep the desk between us. Boyle's gun is lowered, but he still holds it at the ready, his finger on the trigger.

"Then why?" I ask, but somewhere deep in my lizard brain I already know the answer, and as it seeps into the rest of me, so does a chill.

"It's just as Boyle said. You don't find Miser--he finds you."

I can't believe it. I've been used. Maybe from the very beginning. This was never about second chances; the Syndicates don't give them. I was just a pawn in a sick man's game.

I won't be able to save my Lilly after all. I'll die twice, and it will all have been for nothing.

"Don't feel so bad," Fauks says. Still all smiles, he reaches under the desk. There's a click, and the red emergency light ceases to blink. "You've actually done me a huge favor. I was looking for disloyalty in my ranks, and you've helped me find it. Dead or alive, you've proven yourself useful. Smart, capable, violent... very useful."

That final word draws me out of my shock. Useful is... good. I recall that last vision of my daughter, asleep in her hospital bed. "What are you saying?" I ask.

"I'm saying, how would you like to make a new deal?"

I look at my hand again, the animatronic left. I want to make a fist, but I can't quite bring myself to do it. I drop it to my side.

"Where do I sign?"

<hr>

Thomas J. Griffin is a life-long fiction lover and sumo wrestling enthusiast who lives in Nashville, Tennessee and writes out of an attic that could use more natural light. He is the editor of Flash Point SF and his own stories have appeared in such publications as Daily Science Fiction, Martian Magazine, The Arcanist, and elsewhere.

Seeing the Stars

Rick Danforth

Day 1

"Thirty days until oxygen depletes," said the computerised voice that was so infuriatingly calm Sophie wanted to throw water at the speaker to shut it up.

Instead, she asked, "How many days until the *Shapash* reaches its destination?"

"Thirty-five days."

Sophie turned to the girl she had woken up next to, crammed into her single occupancy cryopod. A girl who hadn't been there when she went to sleep. The girl who Sophie had panickily shoved out of the pod and into the hanger to reveal their new nightmare. Trying to process it through the sleep induced mental fog while their ship-issued jumpsuits dripped cryofluid on the deck. "You killed me. You fucking killed me. What did I ever do to you?"

"I'm sorry, I'm so sorry," said the waif of a girl, retreating into the corner between wracking sobs.

"Why would you do such a stupid thing?" demanded Sophie, only just stopping herself from grabbing the girl and bashing her against the monogrammed Shlock Space logo on the sleek metal bulkhead.

"I didn't want to die on Earth with the rest of them."

Protestations died in Sophie's throat. It was hard to say you thought someone should die in Earth's final moments. Even if they had inadvertently killed you. All she could say was, "But why me?"

"You were small," said the girl between stammers and tears. "I needed a pod I could squeeze into."

"Great," said Sophie with a scream, the anger returning to her like a boomerang. Gazing up and down the hall of identical glass and chrome pods that sat humming away, almost mocking her under the lazy, yellow, electric light. "That fat bastard over there lived because of greed. I die due to being eco-friendly and enjoying running."

"I'm really sorry, I never meant to hurt you."

"Now we both die because you didn't want to die alone. Thanks so much for bringing me along."

The girl collapsed into a ball, crying and apologising. Sophie flung her head back in frustration. It was hard to yell at a crying, apologising person. Hopefully, she would stop so Sophie could yell some more later.

It was a lot to take in, being woken early and consigned to death with some stranger in the metal confines of a colony ship, with only the smell of disinfectant and the humming of machinery for company. Sophie considered dragging the girl by her hair to an airlock, throwing her out now. Stopping the problem at its root. There was enough oxygen for one of them, not both. And why shouldn't it be Sophie's oxygen?

But she couldn't do that, she hated herself for thinking it. She couldn't kill spiders, before they died out, how could she kill a woman? No, she corrected herself, a girl.

Instead, she said, "I'm going to my room to sleep."

"Where do I sleep?" asked the girl, between sobs.

"Take the pod, given you wanted it so much." Sophie walked away before she apologised, she shouldn't have to apologise. The girl had killed her. Unless she sacrificed herself to save Sophie, but based on the evidence available it felt unlikely.

In a daze, Sophie navigated the warren of identical metal halls with the confidence of a hundred induction videos with mandatory tests. All essential or her ticket would have been revoked. Flashing her wristtab to open the door, she entered what was less of a cabin and more of a cell.

Enough room for a cot, bed and sink. Any spare space was filled with the feeling of ominous dread. But it left just enough room for echoes to bounce around as Sophie cried herself to sleep.

She'd just wanted to see the stars.

Day 2

Sophie must have drifted off, as she was woken by a knocking on the door. She tried to ignore it, but it was the gentle, consistent knock of someone who intended to be there for a while.

For a second Sophie wanted to let the girl knock until her knuckles bled, but she pushed that thought away. It was petty and vindictive. And as a petty and vindictive person, Sophie had to work very hard to not appear to act like one.

She opened the door, revealing the waifish girl stood trying to look small. It didn't take much work. Even in the narrow metal passageways that reeked of ammonia deep clean.

"I'm sorry. I didn't mean for this to happen to you."

"That *really* fixes everything," said Sophie, unable to hold back the sarcasm. But she didn't hit her, so that had to count as neutral at worse. "Now we've got past that, why don't we go out for ice cream as we slowly wait to die."

"If you want to push me out of the airlock, I understand."

"Please, don't tempt me," said Sophie, her eyes already shooting to the direction she knew the airlock resided in. A mere two hundred yards away. Ten minutes of screaming and dragging and it could all be over. The earth and the society that went with it was gone, who cared if Sophie threw the brat out the airlock? One burst of energy and then she wouldn't die on the very ship that was meant to save her.

"But before you do, I'm Aisling. What's your name?"

"Sophie."

"Before you kill me, can you show me where the food is? I'm starving."

At that point, Sophie relented. The girl probably weighed eighty pounds tops. Her face was sunken, dehydrated behind a crop of unmanaged, red hair. Halfway between girl and ghost. If she hadn't eaten for a week, Sophie could believe it.

They walked silently towards the canteen, Aisling having enough sense not to push Sophie with conversation. The continuous acceleration of the ship provided half a g of thrust. It was enough to make gravity work, but still made Sophie feel like she was about to fall at any second as she followed the green line to the canteen. She tried not to focus on the red line to the airlock.

Canteen was a grandiose term for a large, featureless room with metal chairs and one vending machine in the middle, but it had a monopoly on the ship. Sophie ordered two Nutri-Goo tubes from the machine, noticing Aisling staring at her wristtab. The girl would probably come steal it in the night, like she had stolen her life.

And in return, Sophie passed her a tube of Nutri-Goo, a thick paste that squirted out of a tube directly into her mouth. It tasted of disappointment rather than the strawberry promised, but was enough to keep them alive. For thirty days at least anyway.

Aisling gobbled it down like it was the first thing she'd eaten in days, which Sophie realised it was, technically speaking. Part of Sophie begrudged her every bite, and every breath of oxygen.

But a bigger part, although not much bigger, made her stand up and get the girl another tube of Nutri-Goo.

Aisling's eyes widened in surprise as she moved suddenly then stopped herself from jerking the tube out of Sophie's hand. Taking it softly, and bowing her head. "Thank you. You're so kind."

"It's a free tube of tasteless goo," said Sophie, scoffing to hide her awkwardness at the thanks. "It's not a pizza."

Not that Aisling seemed to mind. "I've never had a pizza."

"I haven't since they cracked down on the dairy industry." Sophie sighed. It had been the first to go when the blights and smogs slowly killed earth's farms. "One of the things I was looking forward to in the colony was having proper grown food. Not just tubes."

"I've never had any non-synthetic food."

"How old are you?"

"Eighteen," said Aisling.

Sophie had her doubts, but decided not to question it. In any case she was busy doing the maths. Synthetic food pastes had arrived as regular food prices shot up about thirty years ago. Then everyone started saying how regular food wasn't eco-friendly with their dwindling resources, and it became the reserve of the wealthy and for special occasions.

Finally, it was outlawed altogether maybe twenty years ago. By the time Aisling was old enough to eat solids, the only solid was Nutri-Goo, a flavoured paste formed from kudzu. Unless you wanted to pay car sized sums for bootlegged food likely to give you e-coli anyway.

In contrast, Sophie had once eaten so much pizza she'd thrown up. Then ordered another, blissfully unaware of how excessive it would seem later. Something she felt too embarrassed to share with Aisling.

As Sophie realised her initial panic had died down, she decided to double check their situation. Computers made mistakes. As she was more than aware, she had been the technical lead for the systems design on the ship. A position that had granted her a heavily discounted ticket. Alongside other benefits she tried not to focus on. She sat at the nearest terminal, scanned her wrist on the machine, and started typing.

Aisling was watching her like a now-extinct hawk over her shoulder. "What are you doing?"

"Scanning the computer to double check what is happening."

Aisling nodded, watching Sophie's fingers dance. Sophie resisted the urge to hide her wristtab from the girl, the only thing confirming her status to the computers as passenger and not a stowaway like Aisling.

The maths was nauseatingly simple. The Ship had exactly the amount of Oxygen held on board before it left earth, it wasn't designed to clean or scrub the air. And they would run out at thirty days before arriving at the colony in thirty-five days. To ensure air for survival, they needed to be down to one breathing person by twenty-seven days. There was no give in the maths, only in the squishy people who had to breath what little air they had. If they didn't work out a solution in twenty-seven days, then neither of them would make it to the planet to land.

Sophie swore, resisting the urge to kick the harsh metal wall. "The maths checks out."

"I hate maths."

"No, you don't."

"It's killing me, I hate it."

"Maths isn't killing us." Sophies sighed. "It's some crappy accountant who tried to save money by declaring no oxygen reserves an acceptable risk."

Sophie wondered who made that decision? How much did it save? Ten, twenty thousand dollars for some scrubbers? Hell, if they'd just packed some oxygen candles away it could have saved them both. A single human life for one crate of candles. Cheap as hell, all things considered. "Money's all that counts. We're just a line on a spreadsheet."

"You are." Aisling bit her lip and looked away. "I won't be on the spreadsheet."

Sophie shifted uncomfortably at the topic they needed to discuss, but how did one go about it? "Did you lose the lottery?"

"I didn't play." Aisling looked around the room, everywhere but at Sophie. "I wasn't eligible."

"Defects?" asked Sophie, surprising herself by her lack of decorum. But then she supposed she didn't mind making the woman who killed her uncomfortable.

"I'm a bit short-sighted. I shouldn't be doomed to die for that." Aisling looked at her tube and squeezed the last little bit out. "Not like I had the money or a skill anyway."

Now Sophie felt uncomfortable. She remembered the riots on the news when they announced the lottery and the rules, how she had called them selfish idiots. That if they had wanted tickets, they should have got good jobs to pay for the tickets, with a skill that was valuable for the mission. Suddenly, it felt much more reasonable. Nausea rose in her stomach as she tried to forget that the lottery had awarded a surprising quantity of Shlock staff with tickets. Half of her department had won, an interesting amount given the official acceptance odds of 0.1%.

Finally, Sophie came to the realisation that there was a problem to fix. That was her job. She certainly couldn't fix awkward conversations, but she was an engineer, a person who fixed problems. "We either need more oxygen, or less people breathing it."

"Can we go back in the pod?"

"No." Sophie sighed. "Shlock Space automated the on-boarding process to ensure that no-one was swapping people out of pods."

"What about the oxygen for the pods?"

"It's in fluid form," said Sophie, remembering the awkward jingle and cartoon figure from the instructional. And trying to forget initially going to sleep in the fluid felt like drowning.

"Can't we just use that?"

"There's the correct amount for the passengers on board. If you want to use some, you'd have to go through the crew manifest and pick who you want to perish for us to survive."

Aisling hunched over as if sick, like Sophie had thrown the full weight of her decisions at her.

Sophie paused and checked something on screen. "That is actually why we woke up. Thanks to you, we burned through the supply too quickly." Another couple of buttons indicated that they had even used up the entirety of the ship's legally mandated reserve, the only reason they made it this long. Any technical errors with other crew and they'd have a third person awake, with the additional headaches that created.

Another awkward silence, they were almost becoming a theme. Sophie was going to have to find some music for them to listen to if this continued.

"Can we make more oxygen?"

"No, the ship isn't designed for that. it's heading to an atmosphere rich world, so it will just open the doors when it arrives and voila."

"Plants!" Aisling smiled, her eyes lighting up with a spark that Sophie would find endearing in any other person alive. "There are seeds in the hold, right?"

"Correct, but no soil. And we have no way of getting to the hold. The two are unattached so if there is a disaster and the passengers die, they still have cargo to sell to colonists at the other end."

"What abo—"

"There is no way to create oxygen on the ship." Sophie sighed and massaged her head. Maths had always been fun for her, but these numbers hurt to look at. "All we can do is reduce the demand."

"Reduce the demand? You mean…" Aisling swallowed, the cheer draining from her face.

"Yes. One of us will have to take a walk." Sophie shrugged her head at the airlock. Decorated with red signs and a button with yellow and black stripes, as if she needed reminding of the impact.

"How do we decide?" asked Aisling, taking a step back from the airlock as if Sophie would force her through it any second.

Sophie bit down her response that Aisling should go take a walk. It was Sophie's damn ticket.

But looking at Aisling, her thin malnourished frame, how could she say that? You needed money and a useful skill for a ticket.

The young woman before her had never had a chance at either. While Sophie had had an employer which rigged a fifty-fifty ticket chance. It was a problem that Sophie didn't even know how to solve. Not beside her inbuilt desire to scream, and shout, and bully the girl until she did the decent thing.

But she pushed that down, pinching her leg to calm herself, and said, "Why don't we settle in and relax. And tomorrow we can debate it? Not like a day will matter."

"Okay," said Aisling between racking breaths. "What do we do now?"

The SCS *Shapash* had a full complement of multiplayer video games and recreational activities for its role as a homebase on the colony it would help found. Unfortunately, all relied on the locator tag that members wore on their wrist. A film was an option, but Sophie needed something to physically do. Or her thoughts would just spiral.

The best Sophie could do was salvage random items to scratch a chessboard together. Which felt eerily appropriate under the circumstances.

Day 3

"Look. You can't beat around the bush anymore." Sophie fixed Aisling with a stern look, she had been dodging the issue for an hour. "I need an answer, and I need it now."

"Fine." Aisling rolled her eyes and sulked like the teenager she still was, but she moved her pawn. Before being pressed into service, it had been a metal bottle top.

Chess hadn't stopped, they had little else to do, but the conversation had started. Under a veneer of calm that almost wracked Sophie apart, she wanted to scream and shout about how utterly unreasonable it was.

But instead, she moved a rook forward and said, "I've achieved so much. I was Technical Lead for Schlock, I have a master's degree, I won awards for design."

"I'm young. I have a work ethic, maybe I can do better? And I have far more years left to do it in."

"Hmm." Sophie paused, wondering if there was any established testing metric for potential that was actually accurate. She had to force herself not to rise at the age comment. Fifty was now uncomfortably close.

Aisling moved a knight, a bottle top with a scratched 'k', and started a new offensive. "It wasn't my generation who ruined the planet."

"It wasn't mine. Well..." Sophie paused, they had agreed to be as honest and fair as possible. "We didn't help either."

"Exactly, why should I be punished for a failure that happened before I was born?"

"We built the ships and the pods to save the human race?" offered Sophie, mentally adding, "Or some of them anyway."

"If you cut me with a knife, you don't get rewarded for putting a plaster on it afterwards."

"It's better than leaving you to bleed out on the floor?"

"And even better not to cut me in the first place."

"Hmm." Sophie was slowly coming to realise how long it had been since she had spoken to someone with different viewpoints. She wasn't just out of practice with debate, she was terrible at it.

Sophie's queen forced Aisling's king into a trap. After swearing, Aisling began to reset the board. "What about an induced coma?"

"How would we do that?"

"I could bash you over the head?"

"Let's leave that in the backup plan column." Sophie massaged her temples. They had twenty days left, and until then, they had chess. Chess and thin metal walls that kept them trapped like the prisoners they were.

Day 5

Sophie regretted teaching Aisling chess. She was already down to making idle chit-chat to distract the girl.

Aisling just seemed to soak up knowledge like a sponge. After so many years deprived of knowledge, she was consuming gambits and defences that Sophie couldn't match. They watched the same how-to videos on the ship's limited documentary library, but it just seemed to click faster for the girl.

"Does this ship have an escape pod?" asked Aisling.

"No. Not unless you make one yourself, and even if you managed that there'd be the atmosphere from in here so not better off. You'd just be making yourself a coffin." Sophie chuckled, and then saw the stony expression on Aisling's face. They definitely didn't share the same dark humour that Sophie thrived on.

After an awkward silence that lingered like a bad smell, and a seismic level destruction of Sophie's most recent defence, Aisling asked, "What were you excited for most about the colony?"

"Soaking in the sunlight," said Sophie without hesitation. "I miss it."

"I've always wanted to see sunlight."

"You haven't?"

"The smogs formed the year before I was born."

"Ah." Sophie felt awkward, another avenue of connection taken away from her. They really had nothing in common at all. Except the depleting oxygen they were begrudgingly sharing. "You'd like it, I think. It's something you don't appreciate while you have it, but when it

goes away you miss it. Except the sunburn."

"Sunburn?"

"If you spent too long in the sun, it damages your skin temporarily."

"That sounds terrifying," said Aisling, eyeing the dim yellow bulbs overhead as if they may hurt her too.

"It's oddly not." Sophie smiled at childhood memories of foregoing maternal advice of lotions and paying the price. She would have killed to replace the bleach smell on board with that tang of sun lotion. "You know the silliest thing about this?"

"Hmm?"

"My entire life I'd always wanted to see the stars, like the astronauts when I was a kid. I really hoped I'd get chance here. Then they didn't put a single bloody window on the ship."

"You can see them on the monitor?"

"Just like I could on earth." Sophie sighed, looking at the metal wall with longing. One criticism she would send to Shlock was about some posters or windows to change up the view. "But hey, beats doing work, right?"

Sophie laughed. A laugh that stopped when she realised Aisling wasn't laughing. Of course she wasn't, she had no reference point.

Instead, Aisling asked, "You didn't like work?"

"Well…" Sophie trailed off, finding a way to complain about such a privileged position without complaining about it. Maybe twenty percent of people were lucky enough to get a job, and it had been a while since she had spoken to one who hadn't. Who didn't live in the nicer housing areas jobs afforded. "It's not all fun and games. A lot of hard work."

"But the money, the privilege," said Aisling, with little dollar signs in her eyes.

"And it must be pleasant to have a purpose."

"Yes," said Sophie quickly, never once had she thought of it as a purpose. More of a grind. But why ruin the girl's dreams? She had enough misery in her life.

"What was it?"

"I was Lead Systems Engineer for Shlock Space," said Sophie. Seeing Aisling's confusion, she added, "Programming. I designed the computer systems."

"That's incredible. I applied for the degree at Adaptive College, but I was just put in the queue."

"What's the waiting list now?"

"About forty years."

"Ah." Sophie gulped. She had heard about that. It could be a real bind for that, unless your mum happened to work at the university. In which case names got shuffled along in a convenient manner. Well, convenient for Sophie at least.

"I probably wouldn't have done well anyway."

The futility of the statement triggered something in Sophie she thought had been dead for years. Outrage at rolling over and playing dead. "Would you like to learn?"

"What? But I can't use the ship's systems?"

"I have a laptop with me. It doesn't have much use and it can't talk to the ship, but you can use it to learn programming if I set you up with some guides."

It was an old, battered laptop with a dent from where she dropped it rushing out of the car for work, and a weird smudge from what she hoped was a coffee stain. But Aisling loved it so much that she forgot to eat her dinner, and Sophie retired to watch an old movie alone.

Which she ignored, and fell asleep thinking about how on earth they could decide an impossible situation.

"How does it work?" asked Sophie, leaning over Aisling's shoulder as she crouched over the battered laptop.

Aisling demonstrated. She typed in, 'cheese., and the little rat on screen said, "Hurrah."

She typed in, 'no cheese', and the little rat, "Boo."

Aisling's smile drained. "It's rubbish, isn't it?"

"Well…" Sophie paused, stuck between wanting to cheerlead and be honest. "A little bit. But being rubbish at something is the first step to getting better at it. And it's far superior to the first thing I did. That was just 'hello world'."

"Really?"

"Yes. it was an absolute mess." Sophie chuckled. She'd had a very different experience, sat in a classroom with twenty other students as a tutor gently guided them through it. A far cry from a battered laptop with a grumpy, middle-aged woman. "But that's enough for today, you can do more tomorrow."

"I can keep going."

"You'll burn yourself out," said Sophie, frowning as she realised it had taken two weeks to turn into her own mother. "How about dinner and a film?"

As they walked to the canteen, the inevitable arose. It always came back, like a fly around a bad smell.

"Will any family miss you if you pass?" asked Aisling. "You know, at the colony."

Sophie didn't break a stride. "Parents passed away."

"No partner?"

"I was married for a while, but it didn't work out," said Sophie, with the understatement of the year.

"Why?"

"We bickered, we argued. We were too difficult. She wanted kids, and I didn't. We even disagreed about coming on this. She said I just wanted to run away from my problems, and I felt that a dying earth was a good thing to run from." Sophie sighed. Ten years compressed into three sentences probably wasn't much of a marriage anyway. She failed her wife like she'd failed everyone in life. "You?"

"Moments of quick release, but never anything serious."

Sophie twitched uncomfortably, the talk making her uneasy. "How about that dinner?"

Today was a lovely tube of almost beef-like paste, and a documentary on sea-shanties. What a way to spend your final days. Avoiding talking about the elephant in the room, with dinner and a film. Just like her ex-wife used to make.

Day 20

Sophie spent the next morning alone. She checked on Aisling, giggling to herself as she noticed the girl passed out next to the laptop.

She must have stayed up all night programming.

They've only known each other a little while, but there was a strange sense of belonging. Two people inextricably tied to each other in such a macabre way was a bond that very few would ever share. They just fitted together nicely, like two puzzle pieces.

Which was why Sophie found herself pouring over the computer for the umpteenth time. Rechecking the figures until they were meaningless. And then checking through every part of the ship's inventory. Aisling watched her over her shoulder, almost mesmerised by Sophie's frantic clicking and scrolling.

The ship didn't cooperate willingly, but Sophie didn't ask nicely. She designed these systems, from top to bottom. And half the passwords weren't even changed from the default admin.

She smashed the lists wide open like her own personal piñata, checking everything from personal effects to the first aid kit. Valiantly searching for fail-safes and backups that should exist. There should have been possibilities— possibilities other than the company literally cost cutting a person to death. In all that data, in all the miles of ship, there should be a happy ending.

Bugger that, Sophie corrected herself. This shouldn't have been an ending at all. There should have been enough space on the flight. Hell, they shouldn't have had to evacuate a planet at all.

But they were here now, so 'shouldn't' had no meaning.

Sophie paused, eyes twinging, as the numbers started to blur into one meaningless block. She'd forced herself to look at every option, every corner, but the only thing she found was pain in numeric form.

"We could both die?" offered Aisling, stumbling on the words.

"What?"

"That would be fair?"

"And futile." Admitting that she wished she could accept it made her throat raw. "If we had one chocolate bar and couldn't decide who got it, we wouldn't throw it in the bin. It would be a waste."

"We could share a chocolate bar, we can't share this for much longer." Aisling swallowed. "I don't want to die, but I don't want you to die either."

"We'll figure something out."

"How?" Aisling placed a firm but gentle hand on Sophie's shoulder. "We've been over it a million times and you have nothing."

"Something always comes up, just like in the films. I'll find it."

"If you say so."

"I know so," lied Sophie. The machinery hummed tunelessly, and she pulled her hair hard enough to break several stands. "I'll have a think. There has to be a solution. Now don't you have some work to be doing?"

Aisling demonstrated the database model she had been working on, getting so excited that she forgot about their debate. Asking inane questions about key value pairs like that was remotely important in their situation. Sophie couldn't have been more thankful.

She noticed neither mentioned another way of deciding, they couldn't think of any. And didn't want to.

Day 24

The idea had been discussed, emotion had drained. It was increasingly hard to pretend the issue could be solved.

There was a lot of data, and Sophie could almost recite it blind. Going over it had become meaningless.

Aisling knew it too, it's why they sat there in silence. With nothing else to talk about or discuss. They knew everything about each other, from Sophie's fused ankle to Aisling's grass allergy. It has been such a short time together, but Sophie felt closer to her than she had to anyone in her entire life. Already she wondered how she could cope with an Aisling sized hole.

As she pondered yet another question she didn't know how to answer. The only kind she seemed to be finding nowadays.

"You know," said Aisling, with a maturity that Sophie envied. "We could leave it to the last minute and flip a coin?"

"We can't leave it to chance. That's absurd," said Sophie. Although part of her relished the easy way out. Keeping herself alive while not having to betray the only friend she'd had in a decade. She could tell herself it was the coin, not her.

"We have two days left, do you have a better idea?"

"Something will—"

"No, it won't." Aisling cupped Sophie's hands in her own. "We both know it won't. You know what you're doing, and even you can't find an answer no matter how hard you look."

Sophie looked to her shoes, finding the worn plimsolls very interesting. "We don't have a coin."

"Now *that* is solvable." Aisling's face brightened. "I can make something on the laptop?"

"Why don't you get to work making us one then," said Sophie holding back tears. Anything to buy some time, even a day.

"On it." Aisling was already moving away. "Should I make a graphical coin as well to view?"

"Yes. That would be lovely."

Aisling jumped onto her laptop, typing furiously like she was tap dancing on an anthill. With nothing better to do, Sophie turned back to the maths and numbers in front of her. Staring down the smoking barrel of the inevitable maths, staring down the long line of items and inventories that can't help her at all. Not unless someone secretly smuggled a hundred oxygen candles in their jumpsuit.

She pauses, eyes unfocused, staring into her screen until the numbers blur and run. She's put enough pain and discomfort into this. And she knows that's all she will get back.

Turning it off, she opened a view of the stars ahead of them. Even on a computer screen they were beautiful, the blanket of twinkling stars stretching to infinity. All she wanted was her childish dream to see them, and this is how it ended up.

Sophie helped Aisling with a minor query, telling her how proud she was of her start to programming. Then she sniffed at a Nutri-Goo and then eventually managed to cry herself to sleep.

Day 25

After a night of sleeping like a baby, nothing but endless crying and kicking, Sophie staggered into their little living room. There was no sign of Aisling, but the laptop was on the side. Hundreds of lines of code were there, just waiting for the compile button.

Sophie gave a grim smile as she saw Aisling is delaying the inevitable. The software was written, but the girl couldn't bring herself to press compile. Despite staying up late into the night to craft it.

In her youth, a time that felt it was black and white, Sophie remembered working through the night. Even going as far as to building her own computers. Before the joy faded, and it became just another task like cleaning the house. Sophie didn't want to see that in Aisling. It would come eventually, it always did. Although it probably wouldn't before they landed on the colony.

Something about that hit Sophie hard. Before she knew it, she was walking down the ominous red line towards the airlock. That realisation was the straw that broke the camel's back, there were just so many things the girl would never get the chance to experience. So few rewarding memories.

Sophie had been given a first-class ticket through life as she floated along in a happy warm stream in a doughnut of comfort. It was hard to justify a second

one when it could go to somebody who could do so much more with it.

Sophie tried not to focus on the finality of her decision, instead focusing on the positives. On what Aisling would gain. Memories of sunlight, physical food and hopefully a fulfilling programming job. That Sophie would no longer have to see this bare metal prison. Instead, she smiled, she'd finally get to see the stars.

As she got to the airlock, Sophie paused as she found Aisling sleeping in a pile of blankets in front of it. Sophie stopped breathing for a moment, then smiled. Aisling already knew her so well, she'd predicted what she would do. It would be touching if it wasn't problematic.

But this was a problem Sophie could solve. She used her bootlaces to tie Aisling's hands and feet together as softly and quietly as she could manage. Then taking a deep breath, she grabbed Aisling's feet and ran ten paces down the corridor, dropped her, and sprinted to the airlock.

The door was already closing before Aisling registered what was going on, and locked before she worked her hands free, screaming, "No! Don't you dare!"

The airlock interior door closed with a clank. A small blue light illuminated on a panel. No doubt about what that does. Sophie smiled, the stars were so close. Halfway there.

<maybe<

Aisling stopped panicking, and smiled. "Sophie, you did it."

"I'm trying to."

"The extra air in the airlock. It won't have been in the ship's sensors."

Sophie said, "Computer, how long can I survive on air in the airlock?"

"Three hours."

"Sorry." Sophie really was. "Life just is never that neat." >>

"This isn't fair!" screamed Aisling. Which Sophie found ridiculous, nothing in the younger woman's life has ever been fair, but it's probably not the time to argue. "Stop it! Stop it right now! You can't do this!"

"Again, I think you'll find I can." Sophie grinned. "I've made my decision. It's okay. In fact, I've never been more sure in my life."

Sophie just wished she could leave a lingering goodbye kiss on her brow, but she knows to open the door is to admit defeat. Instead, she takes off her wristtab, and ties it on a pipe. Aisling will need it later.

Right now, she claws at the panel on her side of the airlock, but she can't stop it once started. Amusingly the safety mechanism was there to stop someone in the ship from flushing someone out of the airlock against their will. Although maybe only Sophie can enjoy that irony.

"But it was my fault," said Aisling between sobbing, panting tears.

"Wanting to live isn't a fault. Goodbye, Aisling." Sophie smiled, blew a kiss, and then went to see the stars.

Rick Danforth lives in Yorkshire, where he works as a Systems Architect to fund his writing habit. He has had several short stories published in a variety of venues including Etherea and Translunar Traveler's Lounge.

Flying Takes Heart

Adrienne Canino

The dragon saw a ridge of mountains that plunged into icy ocean water. She decided this was the spot. Not too high up. Not too far down, either. Contrary to popular belief, she did not like heat much.

No one really noticed as she settled herself between ridges, over the cold, pebbly beach where her skin blended in instantly. At least, no one said anything. She stretched her talons into the earth, tail curled up like a cat, wings arching for a brief moment against the night sky. Then she folded them up and laid her bones to rest among the new mountain range, neck extended just enough to watch the sunsets over the ocean.

Cruelly, her life continued. Quietly, she just watched it go by.

She laid for so long that little bits of earth gathered about her, the beach not caring about its new inhabitant. Water pooled in the niche her tail made against her side, a small pond that attracted beavers. Birds began to land on her back, scratching or nesting. Soon woodland creatures found their way there as well, with the porcupine perhaps knowing it was her underneath. She lay for so long that ferns and flowers began to sprout on her skin.

Still, the dragon refused to get up, waiting for the day her breath would go with the sunset.

And eventually trees and berries grew over the ferns and flowers. Larger and larger creatures made their home along her back. Her eyes dulled as decade after decade, she watched.

They all forgot there had ever been dragons.

One day people came to the mountain range.

They did not know it was a new mountain range, only that it looked like home. They scaled her sides and set up camps. They huddled in the lee between her forearms and made use of the pond her tail had collected.

The dragon remained, mute and motionless.

The people stayed for more than one moon. Then they stayed for more than two moons. The dragon lost count after that.

The people grew older, but there came to be some young ones too, hatchlings with barely enough bones to stretch out their folds of skin.

One day, such a hatchling was playing precariously close to the ocean, under the guise of collecting driftwood. She puttered about just to the side of the dragon's muzzle, meandering farther and farther onto the mudflats.

But this ocean was notoriously fickle. The dragon knew this, and had come to know a thing or two about hatchlings in her time, too. A bore tide came sweeping in, and none of the people saw the youth on the mudflats on the edge of danger.

So, for the first time in an age, the dragon moved.

As the tide came rippling through, she tipped the very edge of her muzzle, just enough pressure to push the water, disrupt the threatening tide, and knock over a tree. The hatchling scrambled along the tree, through the mud and up the slope, hair and tears streaming out behind, driftwood forgotten.

That evening, as the dragon watched the sunset, an eagle circled down and down and down to perch on that fallen tree.

"I saw that," she said.

The dragon said nothing, still and silent as the sky.

"My mother told me stories about this place. Stories her mother had told her. I had never really believed her," the eagle added.

The dragon watched the glowing orange sun drop into the mirrored water.

The eagle flew away.

The people celebrated the hatchling's close escape from the tide, praising the earth for the quake and leaving flower wreaths and shiny shells at the base of the fallen tree.

As if the earth had done the hard work.

That winter started early, and extra cloudy this year. The mountaintops, then the top of the dragon's body, then even the pond in the protected shelter of her tail, accumulated feet and feet of snowdrifts.

Some of the older people had a lot of trouble with that much snow. The dragon was a little older herself, so she could tell.

There was one avalanche that pushed the snow through the trees fencing it in, right over the path the people used to get to the glacier lake on the far side of her rump. It was a narrow path between herself and another young mountain, and even though the snow could be packed down, the ice sheet on top was the true problem.

Going to ice fish on the lake was one of the ways some of those older people kept busy in this slower season, the younger ones on hunting expeditions or busy with the lumber work. The fishing was good for food, but better for their dignity, and the dragon saw this too.

So, she flicked her tiniest back talon, a little up and to the side.

Nearly a century had created a sizable accumulation of earth and scree about her resting place. The gravel she scattered into the air tumbled against the mountainside, and onto the path. It broke up the ice, and kept the surface from being too slick. If they were careful, the older people could just make it.

And they did, talking and laughing and making fun of themselves for needing their walking sticks. They passed carefully and safely along the gully to the lake, a blush of life on their faces.

The night before springrise, the eagle flew down to the dragon again.

"I saw that," she said.

The dragon remained soundless as

snowflakes.

"I wish they had shared some fish with me," the eagle sighed, and settled in to watch the sunset.

That spring was busy. The people had been building boats all the time, all the seasons they had stayed with her. They were good boats, sometimes bark wrapped frames that looked frail but darted daringly, sometimes stout planks bent around a center mast with a giant sail, puffed up with wind and pride. There were enough boats to carry all the people.

Soon the entire village emptied out. Every person, young and old, paraded down to the coastline. The dragon knew a thing or two about leaving a home behind, so she understood that these people were not planning to come back. They loaded all their things and themselves into the boats on the rocky coastline.

Then, they turned back, looking up the jutty terrain that was the dragon's back.

And they sang.

They sang of miracle earthquakes. They threw flowers. They praised the tiny pond and its busy beaver. They stomped their feet in dance. They recounted the hard winter and the good luck of gravel paths. They sang, and laughed, and wept, giving thanks to a place they had called home.

Giving thanks to the dragon.

Then, one by one, they lifted sail and oar and anchor, and waved goodbye. A high and strong tide arrived to pull them away.

So, the dragon took a deep breath.

It rumbled in her belly, and stretched her ribs, and curled the tongue in her mouth. Trees and dirt and gravel shook. The beaver dam sprung a leak. The animals, except the porcupine, skittered about.

She blew very, very gently, just enough to fill the sails and teeter the canoes, speeding the boats on their way into the sunset.

The people cheered and whooped and clapped.

The dragon was still watching them when the eagle drifted down to her familiar perch nearby.

"I know, I know," the dragon whispered, the rumble shuddering through the stones on the beach. "You saw that."

The eagle paused for a long while, pinks and purples coming into the sunset.

"My mother told me a story once," she finally said. "But I think she was wrong."

The dragon looked sideways at her friend.

" I don't think anyone who has that much love to give, has really given up on anything."

The dragon grumbled so loudly that half the new spring buds on the trees burst into leaf.

"So," the eagle continued slyly. "Do you remember how to fly?"

The dragon looked at the sunset, tiny dots of boats sailing along the brilliantly colored water.

And she smiled, stretching her wings in an earth slide the young mountains would never forget.

"My dear," she whispered. "I was born to fly."

—⸻⟨⬦⟩⸻—

Adrienne Canino lives in south central Alaska and indulges in cozy winter habits most of the year. She has loved sci fi and fantasy since meeting the characters of Ellen Ripley and Diane Sarrasri in her youth, and probably even before. She escapes her day job wrangling research and technology by hiking and camping and writing and reading.

A Calvarial Suffusion of Peace

Jason P. Burnham

Taking photos that decay at the bottom of filing cabinets is my job.

The mother had a chance at her son's killer as she ran across the house toward gunshots. Grabbing the katana over the fireplace, she charged, missing the attacker, but slicing through the gun barrel. Hands stinging from metal-on-metal impact, she dropped the blade and was knocked unconscious.

I photograph the wooden mantle, red-brick fireplace, and family portraits littering the floor. In one picture, the victim looks about eight, just like my son. He and his mother wear baseball caps, grinning ear-to-ear, half-eaten stadium dogs in their laps.

The gun barrel is on the ground too, the fragment's black steel visually unremarkable. It's the first evidence we've had on a case like this in months and something draws my hand toward it.

It's warm through my blue nitrile gloves even though the shooting was hours ago.

I look down the barrel, face-to-face with a metallic countenance no child should see. Inside the barrel is something pink that turns suddenly gray. I probe the material with a gloved finger. It's squishy and recedes when touched, but a small tendril shoots out where my finger had been. I drop the barrel; it lands with a *crack* on the wood.

"Johnson!"

Crime Scene. I swivel to the door.

"Sir?"

"You take *pictures*. You don't *touch*." Vazquez fumes.

I glance from gun barrel to Vazquez. "If I promise to not touch, can I stay?" I'm desperate to know what that *thing* is.

Vazquez places the barrel in a clear plastic bag—*it's empty.*

"If you get out of here *right now*, Lucas, I won't report you for evidence tampering."

It's a thinly veiled threat. "Yeah." I back away slowly. The walls are closing in and fresh air seems warranted.

I try Dr. Ylkovich's centering exercises to get rid of the sinking in my stomach, the feeling of Earth falling away from me. They don't work.

The house is empty—Tess and Isaac are visiting Grandma. It's probably better that way tonight.

Intellectually, I realize food is necessary, but find myself at the computer, frantically scouring photos, news reports, anything for answers to an impossible question—what lives *inside* a gun?

Something scratches inside my skull. I won't sleep until I see that gun barrel again—I have to go back to the precinct.

The evidence desk is unoccupied. Whoever is "on duty" is probably goofing off somewhere.

I walk row after row of open metal shelves; files, folders, forensics, bar-coded and separated by date, section after section of unsolved crimes. I find today's bin. As when Vazquez bagged it, there is nothing inside the gun.

I know what I saw.

I wedge my personal sidearm between two lockers, pick up the katana, and swing it with all my strength.

KLANG. Fierce vibrations radiate to my shoulders and my gun barrel is on the floor—I'm not sure I could have withstood a second attempt.

"Everything okay?" someone calls from the desk with an 'I'm not coming to check it out, even if you say so,' tone.

"Crate fell."

The desk person grunts.

Gloved, I pick up my gun barrel and find a pink-gray blob. I poke it and as it recedes, tendrils shoot toward my finger.

Thank God I'm not hallucinating, but what the hell's God up to? He, She, or They provide no answers. I'd heard gun-cutting was a myth, but maybe this blob weakens the barrel's structural integrity.

Maybe whoever's at the evidence desk can help. It'll require no effort on his part, but that may be asking too much.

"Patrinski, this is from today's case." He doesn't look up so I stare at his pink, bald head. "What's this look like?"

He holds a hand around his magazine without putting it down. He lifts the transected steel to eye level and peers down the shaft.

"Gun barrel." He puts it on the desk and returns to his magazine.

I look again—it's empty.

Bewildered, I stand for a moment at the desk, my presence irking Patrinski into putting down his reading material.

"Shouldn't you be lookin' at *pictures?*"

I know when I'm being told to get lost. "Thanks for the insight."

I leave the precinct. I'm fifty percent sure I'm not hallucinating.

Sun shining through white venetian blinds wakes me. Good thing it's Saturday or I would've slept through my shift, in this cold, wife and alarm clock-free bed. Bunched sheets reflect distressed sleep.

My first instinct is to continue my computer search. I don't remember posting on message boards, but a mailbox full of emails answering the question 'anyone seen something living inside a gun?' suggests I did.

Many responses berate me for owning a gun, which is fair. I hate guns. I didn't want the damned thing—my father bequeathed it to me against vehement protestations. This was its first closet exodus. Two pages into the email queue, one catches my eye—it's the only one with an attachment. The body of the e-mail is one word—*Yes.*

The attachment jolts me upright.

A photo of the pink-gray thing, but it's not my gun. I respond to the email with my phone number.

I distract myself as I wait by looking at pictures of Tess and Isaac above the computer. Tess is proud she and Isaac look so similar. *I grew him, I earned it.* The same brown eyes, wavy brown hair, rounded face and noses. She worries he'll grow a beard when he's older and look too much like me.

I jump when my phone rings.

"Hello?"

"You've seen it?"

"Who is this?" I ask.

"Line's not secure."

What?

"I'll contact you later. Don't tell *anyone*," says the man's voice.

The connection severs. I stare at the darkened phone wondering where dreams and consciousness diverge. Finding no answer in my pale, bespectacled reflection, I plop into the computer chair to find the browser window empty.

All email replies to my message board post are gone.

Dread grabs at my stomach; I need to call Tess.

But the person said not to tell anyone…

Tess says, *I'm not anyone, I'm your wife.* On the other hand, *someone* just remotely deleted my e-mails.

Tess'll be home Monday.

Hopefully I figure this out before then.

I wake in a cold sweat, but it wasn't dreams that awoke me—Tess called three times. I call immediately.

"You better be dead."

"It'd be hard to answer if I was dead."

"Lucas! I've been worried sick!"

"I'm sorry baby. I… had a weird day."

She lowers her voice and I hear her fidgeting with her hair. "Are the anxiety and depression back?"

Dr. Ylkovich said my problem was situational depression from being at murder scenes. My treatment options are to eliminate homicides from society or quit.

"No, it's… just a weird day."

Her voice shifts. "Then pick up your phone!"

There are no excuses without telling her everything. The memories of 'everything' are hazier, more dream-like by the minute. "I'm sorry."

"You better be!"

I quickly change subjects. "How's your mom?"

"She's fed Isaac enough cookies to give him diabetes."

I chuckle. He's a good eater. "What're y'all doing today?"

"Besides eating cookies?" she scoffs. "Ike wants to see penguins at the zoo."

Antarctica has always fascinated him. He's the only kid I know who wants to be a scientist at McMurdo.

"I miss you two."

"We miss you. Sorry you had a bad day."

"I'm off today—time to sit, sleep, and watch TV."

"Expect retribution for this lazing about upon my return."

"Love you, honey."

"Uh-huh. Talk to you later."

Time for breakfast. Maybe greasy protein will clear away the fog.

I head for the kitchen, but the phone rings again. When we started dating, Tess would call back right after hanging up because she 'wanted to say I love you one more time.' It was cute, then annoying, then cute again after she stopped doing it frequently. Our relationship has gotten more business-like—she probably hasn't done it since Ike was a baby. It's cute again.

I swipe to answer without checking the number. "Hey baby, I love you too."

"Shaw Park playground. One hour."

The voice from last night. I pull the phone away, but the call has already dropped.

Do I have a choice?

So much for breakfast.

Shaw Park is ritzy—blue water fountains, streams, gazeboes, White people running, a playground with sand, slides, and see-saws. I dress in brunch-goer business casual and bring a book to combat the creepiness of being by the playground without Isaac. Books make people look less threatening, if it's not the Bible. Fortunately, I don't have to look like a creep for long.

"Lucas, is that you?"

A Latino man in his mid-forties, also in business casual, stares at me. He has long, black hair pulled into a ponytail and large gold rings on both pinky fingers.

Is this him?

"It's me, amigo! Andrés!"

I blink.

"We worked at T-Mobile together!"

I never worked at T-Mobile. Unless… It's code—we talked on the phone, ergo, T-Mobile.

"Andrés! Long time no see! How're you?" We shake hands and one-handed hug tap.

"You know, just spreading the Word."

Is *that* code? He *is* wearing a golden crucifix necklace.

I try my own code. "Bumping into you reminds me. I dropped my phone recently and the parts came out, but the *insides* confused me." Hopefully he knows I'm talking about that pulsating pink-gray *thing*.

His eyes dart from side-to-side—*We can't talk here.* "I know where to catch you up on the latest and greatest in cell phones. Let's head there—I've got connections."

That's that—I'm not sure I like my newfound fatalism.

He unlocks a Prius and despite my instincts, I climb in.

"Pretend you're drinking coffee." He holds out a mug and puts one to his mouth. "They can't hear us, but they can lip read."

I put the… HeatMate, it's called, to my face. I survey the car—clean, excepting a few coffee stains near the cupholders. On the dash, a battery recharge graphic whirls like the gears in my brain.

"The hell is going on Andrés?"

"It's actually Enrico, and what the hell is going on is you've witnessed the parasite."

"The what?" The mug drops from my mouth.

Andrés or Enrico or whoever he is shouts, mug still covering his lips. "*Mug or you don't speak.*"

I raise it and apologize. "I saw the *what*?"

He presses the accelerator. Banks, brunch-goers, and poodles flash past.

"The gun parasite. The parent species is invasive, which is why we have such problems with them."

I put the coffee thermos down—what will it matter if the surveillance crew sees me laugh uncontrollably? When I wipe the last tear of ludicrous laughter away, Enrico still has his mug to his lips.

"You done?"

"You're serious?"

"'Fraid so, *amigo*. Thought you'd understand."

"I thought I was having a psychotic break."

"That's *after* you're infected," he says matter-of-factly.

"Come again?"

"As incidental hosts, humans experience silent cerebral infiltration affecting executive function."

"In English?"

"The gun parasite infects humans and invades their brain, altering decision-making capacity and how they think," says Enrico.

"Why has nobody noticed parasitic brain infections spreading across the US?"

Enrico laughs, a guttural, shaking sound ending in a snort. "Because it just turns them into second amendment supporters."

CRACK.

I shriek, spitting coffee onto the front windshield where it mixes with Enrico's blood and splattered brain.

Enrico's body slumps onto the steering wheel and another bullet cracks the windshield where my head had been before the car swerved.

I grab the wheel and duck out of sight. The back windshield blasts out. Brunch-goers scream on a restaurant patio we've driven into, red cloth umbrellas knocked astray.

The car grinds to a halt over outdoor-seating detritus. Airbags deploy against my head, completing the deafness begun by the bullet barrage. I slump to the passenger door and pry my way onto warm asphalt.

I never should have got in this car.

Restaurant patrons flee and adrenaline propels me. Whoever shot Enrico aimed for me and I have no intention of sticking around to find out who or why.

On all fours, I follow tennis shoes and a pair of khakis. To my left are bare feet underneath a summer dress held at the hem by a fleeing person. To my right are ironwork fences demarcating the divide between patios and street.

Breaking through the veil of silence that is my decibel-assaulted eardrums, I hear sirens, but my feet don't slow. Behind me is never seeing Tess or Isaac again. Ahead is blurry, but no one is shooting from there.

I straighten and speed up, passing barefoot dress hem and khaki tennis shoes.

The shots have stopped, but my feet keep going, my heart racing. Tess and Isaac are getting clearer ahead of me. I don't look back.

"Hello?"

"Darren, it's Lucas Johnson."

Darren was my supervisor before he got promoted to Lieutenant. He's intimidating now—enormous muscles, buzzed short hair, and eyes becoming more piercingly blue with age, a countenance I'm glad to see in the carpool lane and not across an interrogation table. His daughter, Ellen, goes to school with Ike.

"Lucas! To what do I owe the pleasure?"

We bump into each other at school events and promise to hang out, but never do.

"I was wondering," I pause, palms sweating, though unsure why, "Do you have that babysitter's number who used to watch Ellen?"

I glide one hand over cool, marble countertops, first right, then left as I pace a loop around the kitchen. I didn't bother watching the news for a report on the incident, and I hadn't stuck around for the cops. I had needed safety, a clear head, to determine who might have gun parasite information. Hence, Darren's medical student babysitter.

"Ah, what's her name? Kathleen? Katy?"

I laugh politely. "Rachel? I dunno."

Darren chuckles. "You and Tess planning a date?"

"Yeah, *heh*, haven't had one this year."

"Yeah man, I'll text it to you. Y'all okay?"

I sigh, some weight gone from my shoulders. "Just keeping up with Isaac and his extracurriculars. They grow up fast."

"Tell me about it. Ellen has a boy crush."

"Kids." I huff.

Sirens in the background disrupt whatever Darren says and I startle.

"You working? Didn't mean to disturb you."

"No, I'm home." The background sirens are so loud it sounds like the precinct. "But I need to get going. Good hearing from you, Lucas. We should get together sometime."

"Absolutely. Thanks in advance for the babysitter's number."

"No problem. Take care."

Tess and I had heard all about this babysitter at school pickup. In the world of ultra-competitive parents, even your babysitter has to be training to be a doctor.

A text message notification chimes.

Haha her name is Stephanie. Weren't even close.

I tap the contact card for "Stephanie Babysitter" and the phone rings.

Medical school students know about parasites, right?

The dial tone reminds me I should call Tess, but things have got too wild and I don't want to scare her. This is a face-to-face story.

"This is Dr. Rodriguez."

Doctor? How long's it been since Darren told me about her?

"Oh, sorry. This is Lucas Johnson. I..."

"Mr. Johnson, nice hearing from you, though I'm curious how you got my cell. Did you need medication refills or...?"

I'm surprised how calm she is for thinking a patient has got her cell. "Oh, no, Doctor, I'm not your patient. You babysit Ellen, my friend Darren's daughter, and I was wondering if you might be available to watch my son Isaac."

This isn't how I envisioned this conversation.

"I do miss Ellen; she's so sweet. Unfortunately, I'm quite busy at the hospital, working full-time as a doctor."

I sense an impending disconnection. "Can I ask you a medical question?"

A stifled sigh comes through. "Sure, but quickly, I have patients to care for."

"Who might I speak to about unusual parasites?"

"A parasite? Not many of those in America. Do you have a parasite?"

I note a hint of disbelief. "Oh no, I saw it in the environment." Technically true.

"Did you find it on a bird?"

"No, why?"

"Too bad—the university's microbiology lab is doing bird surveys. Anyone finding a dead bird can bring it in for necropsy. They told the hospital about it because occasionally we see patients with avian-related illnesses."

I have an idea.

"That's interesting and I thank you sincerely for your time, doctor."

"No problem. Have a nice day, and good luck."

Click.

I'm gonna need a lot more than luck.

After some sleuthing and a series of phone transfers, I finally reached the bird surveyors lab. They told me a post-doc was on call for sample acceptance and processing, so I wrap my gun barrel in a brown paper bag and place it in a bird-sized shoebox. Hopefully that'll get me in the door.

The car crash is too fresh and the university isn't far, so I pull down my bicycle and put the shoebox in my backpack. I take the scenic route along the tree-lined running path, verdant plants in bloom disturbed by the sounds of cars racing.

I do a double take when I see speeding vehicles over the well-maintained hedges—three black SUVs with tinted windows.

Is someone tracking me?

Deep breath. I'm being paranoid.

But just in case, I stick to the path hidden from the road by trees.

"Nobody's ever asked to watch specimen processing." Dr. Li has black hair in a tight bun, a white coat, and underneath it a shirt that says 'Fowl Play' with birds on a playground.

"Clever shirt." I say, trying to distract from the apparent oddity of my request.

She smiles. "It's from my mom."

I follow her through the maze of the lab.

"You were saying a parasite has been killing birds?" We pass dimly lit labs, equipment on standby mode, walls of lab coats awaiting Monday morning for people to reanimate them.

"It's a possibility. Years ago, birds were dying from eating snails harboring a parasite which caused internal bleeding."

I've come to the right place. "Yikes. Can you identify non-bird parasites?"

Dr. Li stops next to a tall gray machine with a blue cylinder in the middle.

"This machine will identify *any* parasite."

I wring my hands together. "I need to be honest with you."

Dr. Li raises an eyebrow. "Please don't tell me I've made a mistake letting you in."

"I can explain."

She backs away slowly.

"It's not creepy." The fear in her face tells me my meager reassurances aren't working. "Just... let me show you what's in this box."

"Tell me, don't show me," she says nervously.

"You won't believe me if I tell you."

"Mr. Johnson." Dr. Li's thumb is white where it presses hard onto the dead-man switch app on her phone.

My heart races. "It's a severed gun barrel with a parasite living inside."

"You're right; I don't believe you." Dr. Li's hands shake. I feel awful she is terrified, but I'm in too deep.

Slowly, I put my backpack on the floor, extract the shoebox and gun barrel, placing the clear plastic bag on Dr. Li's machine. I step away, hands aloft.

"See for yourself. If it's nothing, you'll have a helluva story about the gun parasite weirdo. I'm very sorry to have scared you."

Seeing the bag really contains only a *piece* of a gun, Dr. Li pulls on a single blue nitrile glove, the other hand remaining on her phone.

When she picks it up and peers inside, she immediately drops it. And her phone.

The shrieking alarm drowns out the crash of the gun barrel.

Dr. Li fumbles with her phone to silence it. "I didn't mean to..."

The blaring alarm quiets as she resets the app. Her phone rings.

"Ms. Li, are you okay?" I hear when she answers.

"I accidentally dropped my phone. I'm okay." Pause. "My verification code is 4478923." Her hands shake as she disconnects.

Dr. Li stares at me, a mixture of fear, curiosity, and resignation. "I'm definitely going to regret letting you in."

Dr. Li furrows her brow at the machine's report. "It's not a good match."

"What's that mean?"

"The machine compares protein signatures. If there's a good match, it will have high certainty about the organism. Whatever *this* is, the certainty score doesn't meet the identification threshold."

"So we can't tell what it is?"

"Kind of—it gives the nearest match— *Cryptotorula neutribacilis.*"

Dr. Li rolls her chair from the gray and blue machine to her computer atop the black lab bench, wooden shelves all around, filled with bottles containing liquids of various colors.

"What're you doing?" I ask.

"Googling it. I'm a *bird* parasite expert. I've never heard of this."

I watch over her shoulder as a small number of search results pop up and she clicks one.

"*Cryptotorula neutribacilis,* ferrotrophic fungus, natural habitat bathypelagic zone hydrothermal vents. Commensal parasite of deep ocean shrimp. Exhibits neurotropism, controlling shrimp migration patterns into iron-dense habitats."

I blink. "What's that mean?"

"It's a deep ocean fungus that uses iron as a nutrient source, which it achieves access to by controlling deep-sea shrimp brains." She exhales deeply. "This is incredible—its main nutrient source is *iron.*"

"And?"

"And it lives in a *gun.* Made partially of iron... This identification has to be right, or nearly so."

My head swims.

Dr. Li taps commands into the identification machine, attaches a USB drive, and transfers it to her computer. She flips through screen after screen of indecipherable squiggly lines.

"What're you doing?"

"Looking for your parasite's protein signature. Maybe somebody's described it before, but it isn't common enough to have made the machine's library of recognized organisms."

Tess and Isaac jump to my mind. They're blurry again, like when I crawled out of the car crash. My legs dance anxiously—I feel like I need to run.

"That's strange," says Dr. Li.

Onscreen, blocks of black and white text are interspersed with squiggly lines like the ones Dr. Li pulled off the machine.

"I found an identical protein spectrum, but apparently the only report of it is this patent document."

"Patent for what?"

"For the organism inside your gun."

I glance at the identification machine and shudder. "You can patent parasites?"

"You can patent any living thing you've bioengineered or genetically modified. Agriculture companies all do it."

My stomach sinks. "Who owns the patent?"

She scrolls through the document.

"The NRA?" My jaw drops.

Dr. Li edges toward the window.

"Who the hell are you? Bringing me an NRA-patented, gun-living, shrimp-brain-controlling parasite?"

With shaking hands, I shove the gun barrel into my backpack.

"Dr. Li, thank you. Do us both a favor—erase this data and pretend we never met."

Dr. Li is nodding behind me, distant as I run from the lab.

I scream at my no-signal, piece-of-crap phone as I emerge into the tree-shaded, fountain-studded courtyard adjacent the lab.

It's dark and the day has cooled—I hadn't realized how long 'specimen processing' had taken.

I need to call Tess—she and Isaac are getting blurrier, darker in my mind's eye.

I'm running to my bike, a thumping sound overhead.

No cell signal.

I trip and fall into the dirt.

Thump thump thump.

A helicopter.

Crunching gravel and floodlights surround me.

Three black SUVs.

Tess and Isaac are shadows in my mind as a heavy weight presses against my back and neck.

"We can't take him in. It's fucking Lucas Johnson. He's one of ours."

My name echoes from deep underwater.

"He can disappear, like the other two."

"No."

Two? Andrés? No… Enrique? Dr. Li?

"You heard the recording. They know."

Recording?

"My kid's friends with his son. We're *not* disappearing him. Just let…"

Let *what* what?

I can't move or speak. Leaden weight presses me…

Where am I?

Light through closed eyes.

Acid stings my face, melting skin away.

My shoulder throbs.

My eyes flutter and two people in unfamiliar uniforms drag a body toward a black SUV.

I'm weightless. Light and sound fade with my consciousness.

I gasp in air, like coming up from a submerged cave.

"Nurse! He's awake."

Whose voice is that? I open my eyes. The room is painfully white with fluorescence. I try to raise my arm to cover my eyes, but lancinating pain stops me. The scent of bleach stings my nose.

"Dar…" I cough.

"They knocked you out to fix your shoulder—you're groggy."

Darren—what are the chances?

"Smells like they bleached my brain."

Darren laughs. "Gotta keep it squeaky clean."

"What happened?"

"Apparently you got mixed up with someone in the park. Ended up in his car, which he crashed. They arrested him and brought you here."

That doesn't seem… right. I remember the park. Then a… lab? Someone taken away in an SUV. Why was I at the park? Meeting somebody I used to work with?

"Why're you here?"

"Heard the APB you were injured; I came immediately."

That makes sense—everyone would know a staff member was down. But…

"Tess."

Darren tosses me my phone. "I knew she'd be worried sick; I texted her from your phone."

"How'd you… get in?"

He smiles. "Lieutenant perks."

I enter my passcode. Sure enough, he texted Tess to say everything is okay.

"Thanks." I grin.

No missed calls from Tess. No calls since… yesterday morning?

"How long was I out? It was Saturday, last I knew."

Darren shrugs. "Six hours? Your shoulder required several reduction attempts because of the previous dislocations."

That seems too long, but why would Darren lie? My shoulder *is* chronically an issue. "Dang thing."

"I'm going to the cafeteria. Want some biscuits and eggs?"

Just what I missed out on yesterday.

"Darn right. Thanks Darren."

"Any time, amigo."

Amigo? Darren never calls me that. Who did?

He closes the door and I stare at my phone. Something's missing, but I can't put my finger on it. The only calls since Thursday are from Tess. Who else would've called? Where would the time have gone?

Darren kindly drops me at home. The ride is amicable, reminiscing about old times at the precinct, discussing what's happening at the kids' school. We promise to hang, maybe get a babysitter so we can have adult fun—he knows one, but can't remember her name, maybe Kathleen or Katy. It's polite, but we both know it won't happen.

My shoulder smarts, but it's functional. I won't lift anything over my head until Tess gets home.

Which should be any minute now.

Where'd the time go? I told her I'd do laundry.

I race to the basement, careful not to slip on the grey-carpeted stairs—I did that once and broke my toe on the metal cabinets at the bottom. I toss clothes into the front-loading washer Tess hates and cycle it. With any luck, this load will be in the dryer when they arrive.

As my feet hit the kitchen's cool, white tiles, gravel crunches in the driveway. I wince—Tess'll forgive me, I hope. I head outside to bring in their bags.

"Daddy!" Ike gives me a giant hug.

"I'm so glad to have you home."

"Glad to be back." Tess pecks my cheek.

Ike lets go. "*I* wanted to stay with Granny!"

Tess gives Ike a side-eye.

I smile, happy to be whole and normal again. The dislocated shoulder and the hospital are fading quickly from memory.

"Granny has better cookies!" complains Isaac.

Tess rolls her eyes and I laugh. "Why don't we go get better cookies?"

Isaac eyes me suspiciously and Tess opens her mouth to say something, but closes it again. Her slouch says, 'I give up.'

"Give me a few minutes of peace. Lord knows I need it."

"Cookies!" Isaac runs down the driveway, light-up shoes flashing.

"Want help with the bags?" I ask sweetly.

"No. Go walk some energy out of that child. The bags aren't going anywhere— I'm gonna lie down."

I kiss her forehead, then grab my wallet. The store's only a block away, so it won't take long.

"Love you," I say to Tess. "Ike! Wait up! I've got the money."

When he realizes cookies are unobtainable without my services, he pauses.

"What kind of cookies are we getting?" I look into his deep brown eyes, Tess's eyes. I can't remember what cookies Granny keeps around.

"You shoulda been there, Dad. Granny's cookies are so full of chocolate they basically explode when you bite them."

"Yeah?"

"They were like *super*cookies!"

"You sure she didn't bake them?"

"You think I wouldn't know about cookies? We bought them together. Trust me; I'm gonna find 'em."

I smile as Isaac bounces ahead, energy bestowed by the promise of sugar-induced dopamine rushes.

The warmth our good time generates lulls me into unawareness and suddenly, a person appears with a clipboard.

Damn. I hate telling these people I don't want to sign their petition.

"Excuse me, moment of your time?"

Unfortunately, I meet their gaze before I can pretend I didn't hear.

"Sorry, we're on a cookie mission."

"Yeah!" agrees Ike.

"Just take a minute, sir." He smiles. "I need support to uphold the second amendment. You support the second amendment, right?"

"Yes, of course," I say.

I sign my name and e-mail on the petition.

"Thank you for protecting America's guns."

I turn to Ike and step toward the store's entrance.

Wait. Something's wrong. Very wrong.

I turn to the solicitor.

"Can I see that again?"

He looks at me funny, but returns the clipboard.

"Ah—it's   @*gmail*.com,   not yahoo.com."

I hand it back and head inside, happy to have corrected the mistake. Wouldn't want to miss e-mails about supporting the ever-important quest to protect America's guns.

The inside of my skull itches, but the sensation lasts only a few seconds before it's replaced by a warmth, flowing up my spine and settling into my brain. A flash of inner turmoil roils through my interstices and just as quickly is extinguished by unparalleled equanimity. Peace fills me, the kind that can only come from giving oneself over completely to a higher power.

Jason P. Burnham loves to spend time with his wife, children, and dog. Find him on Twitter if it still exists at @AndGalen

Watchlist
Reviews

You can tell that we're Trekkies round here because I'm going to rave over *Picard* season 3 and go misty eyed in anticipation for Season 2 of *Strange New Words*, plus I'm going to swiftly pass over the new Star Wars offerings (the *Mandalorian*. Popular. Why? Proper characterisation with the MC hidden behind a mask problematic, *Andor*. Popular. Why? Essentially backstory. Where's the new stuff?)

So on to *Picard*. Oh how sumptuous. Data, Worf, Riker, LaForge, Dr Crusher, Troi and Jean Luc himself back on the bridge of a starship doing 'make it so' stuff, with the added attraction of a kick-ass Seven of Nine and a creepy new villain (shapeshifters – how infinitely flexible). So the gang is (mainly) all back together and while they might look a little greyer and a tad paunchier they've sharpened with age and they slot together like they'd never been away. With a tight script, some great one liners and a significant upgrade to the

CGI this series has come to live in dramatic fashion. This is no longer an extended goodbye to Picard (Patrick Stewart's 82 now, and besides, Marvel need him to play *X-Men* guru Charles Xavier), it's fully fledged Star Trek adventuring in its own right. The current season is, they say, the last one but I can't imagine Paramount will let this lot wander off into retirement again. More!

Elsewhere we've had new seasons of the excellent *Carnival Row* and formerly excellent *Shadow and Bone.* We've been waiting a long time for this second season of *Carnival Row* (since 2019) which killed the momentum of this show – you'd need to rewatch the first season to soak up the rich context – but it's engaging enough. A fantasy tale of exiled Fae folk, boorish humans with a superiority complex and pointless warfare, it's great commentary on colonial stupidity. Orland Bloom and Cara Delevingne are very watchable and my only real complaint is that this series has now wrapped up (which made the ending seem a bit rushed). More!

I'm not so sure I really want more of *Shadow and Bone* though – another fantasy adaptation, this time from Leigh Bardugo's very readable 'Tzarpunk' YA novel series. The first season was very deft and engaging but this time around the characters seem less nuanced, more stereotypical and the action more relentless (and often difficult to follow). It's still beautifully shot with some great core concepts and the occasional really interesting character (I'd pay good money for a thief-adventurer-tortured soul Injej Ghafa spin-of), but I found it hard to immerse myself in the story. The producers obviously expect a new series, though, because there's no tidy *Carnival Row* style wrap up. But will they get it? Don't hold your breath.

Since our last issue we've also been watching *The Last of Us*, or plant-zombies as we like to call it in the Wyldblood offices. For a story based on a video game this one's surprisingly good (and when can you remember anyone saying that about a story based on a video game – *Assassin's Creed*, anyone?). There's a great *Walking Dead* feel to the dynamics of this one – grizzled survivor Joel (Pedro Pascale) and immune-to-infection Elle (Bella Ramsey) on a road trip through post-apocalypse America where a fungus infection turns people into, er, plant zombies. Elle holds the key to a cure – if only nobody kills her first. This is must-watch television – engrossing from beginning to end and (thankfully) renewed for a second season.

On the big screen *Ant Man and the Wasp: Quantumania* belly flopped with some indifferent reviews and poor box-office but had some entertaining one-liners, some classic Marvel action and a new Big Bad – Kang. These films are increasingly looking like poor photocopies but it's entertaining enough for the small screen, which is where it will land any day now. *Fantastic Four* and *X-Men* now please. Stop messing around, Marvel.

Still to come in the near future there's more *Guardians of the Galaxy*, *Aquaman* and *Dune*, plus a new space epic from Zack Snyder called *Rebel Moon*. On TV there's a new series of *Sweet Tooth*, more *Fear the Walking Dead* (sadly the last series), more *Good Omens*, Marvel's *Secret Invasion* and *Loki*, more *Black Mirror*, *The Boys*, *Doom Patrol*. *Severance*, *The Sandman*, *For All Mankind*, *Stranger Things* and *The Umbrella Academy*, plus a load of other stuff and, eventually, David Tennant's (brief) return as *Doctor Who*. And more *Star Trek*. *Strange New Worlds* starts to stream on 15th June, All is well with the world.

Bookworm

Reviews

Just Like Home

Sarah Galley

In *Just Like Home*, Vera Crowder returns to her childhood home to care for her dying mother, Daphne. Their relationship is strained because Daphne blames Vera for the life imprisonment of Francis, Daphne's husband. In a sense, her hatred is justified: Francis helped Vera take the blame for stabbing her friend, Brandon. Yet, Francis was a serial killer who had gotten away with many murders. Vera's act of stabbing Brandon was itself inspired by those murders, which she innocently tried to imitate after watching them from a peephole. Therefore, Francis was indirectly responsible for Brandon's stabbing, warranting his imprisonment. Besides Daphne's hostility, Vera faces discrimination from her hometown, including Brandon, who does not forgive her.

Vera's relationship with her father fascinated me. While tidying the house, she finds pages from his journal, which proclaim his love for her in an emphatic, almost superfluous way. For example, one page reads: "I wonder if she knows I'd do anything for her. I wonder if she understands how I just want to protect her and keep her safe." Ironically, his devotion to her comes into question precisely because it is expressed in such absolute terms. In a previous journal entry, he writes that "she is still just a kid but I've never liked anyone so much as I like her." On one hand, his repeated expressions of love imply steadfastness; on the other, they come across as one-sided and therefore uncompelling. In particular, the word "liked" suggests a reservation in his affection for Vera, revealing a disconnect between the scale of his promises and his actual feelings towards her. Indeed, the first entry ends abruptly with "I hope Vera knows how much I love her and that I'll always". His "love" is only mentioned at the end of his reflection, backgrounded by his nonchalant "like" for her. The incompleteness of his sentence parallels the fragmented nature of his so-called "love", which he can withdraw without warning.

Still, Vera takes Francis' love for granted. As an adult, she does not condemn her father nearly as much as we would expect her to; in fact, she even defends him from the criticism of others. She refuses to see him for the monster he is, because to do so would be to confront the reality that no one has ever loved her. After all, Francis is the only source of affection in her life. Daphne abuses Vera both physically and emotionally. Their visitor, James, is a self-absorbed artist who intends to make Vera his servant. Even Brandon, her childhood friend, ostracises her.

Although the ending seems slightly abrupt to me, Vera's inability to escape the house forms a satisfying parallel with her inability to escape the past, consummating her entrapment. I also find it unnerving that each of the house's inhabitants dies, leaving Vera by herself. Even if she does not share their fate, she must reside in the setting of not only her family's death, but those of the men murdered by Francis. Once again, there is no escape for her.

(Ryan Tan)

Children of Memory
Adrian Tchaikovsky

This is the third in an unnamed series (let's call it the Children novels) from the increasingly prolific Adrian Tchaikovsky set in deep space in the middling to deep future where mankind's managed to spread its self-destruction out to its barely formed colonies leaving behind remnants, e xperiments and new, hybrid forms of life.

The previous instalments, *Children of Time* and *Children of Ruin* introduced most of the cast driving *Children of Memory*. Way back when, scientist Avrana Kern was an early coloniser seeding a virgin planet with genetic modifications, intent in developing sentient helpers for later human colonists. But instead of clever apes she got clever spiders, and in the absence of colonists, an entirely unexpected civilisation. Kern herself lives on until (and through) *Children of Memory*, though whether she's still human though (or AI or something else) is debateable.

Colonists (or refugees) eventually do arrive, having travelled the slow way. Eventually they integrate with Kern and her 'Portids' to an interconnectivity that transforms humans into (capital H) Humans. This odd combination then goes exploring, first finding superbright spacefaring Octopi (also from Kerns genetic experiments) but eventually come across genuinely alien intelligence in the Nodans – parasitic microbes that take over hosts and reshape them.

The Nodan in this story is the human-form Miranda (because, presumably, 'O brave new world, that has such people in't!') trying to make sense of the unfathomable. Kern, Miranda and the others (this time accompanied by sentient birds) have discovered an ancient colony that doesn't appear to have failed (unlike the others). Miranda goes in to investigate and gets drawn into the slow decline of the society she doesn't quite manage to integrate into. But then events get confused and different timelines emerge. She befriends a young girl, Liff, who knows her long dead grandfather, even though the passage of centuries make that impossible. And then there's a witch, deep in a mountain, a dead spaceship in orbit and a slow descent into entropic failure. Miranda tries to make sense of it all, and (of course) the planet, and the colony, are not what they seem to be. All of which gives rise to lots of speculation about the nature of reality and what it is to be human.

This isn't always an easy book to follow, and there was a point where I though Tchaikovsky had spliced together a couple of different drafts and not noticed the continuity problems in the edits, but read through the confusion and it all makes (more) sense. It's pacy, intriguing and dynamic, though it's somewhat soft on characterisation in favour of concept. It ends well, though, and if that's it, that's fine. But I'm a big fan of well written trilogies in four parts so let's hope for more.

(Mark Bilsborough)

Psalms For the End of the World

Cole Haddon

This novel pitches somewhere between *the Matrix* and Marvel's latest take on *Loki,* with more than a hint of Philip K Dick. And it's not averse to taking a sideways lurch into *Titanic* territory just when you mistakenly think the narrative might be starting to make some sense. It's clever, inventive, unsettling and often plain weird.

Grace, a waitress, falls for one of her regulars, Bobby, but Bobby's not what he seems and soon he's wanted by the FBI (who also aren't what they seem, at least not all of them). Bobby can't remember Grace, and he can't remember planting a bomb in Pasadena either. And then he starts to piece it all together…

Oh, but this is a frustrating novel. It took an age to read – not because it's overly long (though it is quite long), and not because the prose is difficult or the writing poor (it isn't, it's silky-smooth and well crafted). It's because structurally, until you reach the end and see how it all twists together like an intricately balanced machine, it comes across as a hot mess (though, in the context of what the story's about, the structure makes perfect sense) with multiple points of view and many diverse scenarios across time and (in some cases literally) space. So you engage with one part then have to shift to another, then another, and by the time you've emerged you can barely remember your own name, let alone some 12th century warrior with a limited shelf life and multiple played out scenarios. Following the thread of anything becomes impossible. So you break off to make a cup of coffee and watch *Ted Lasso* instead. Immersive it isn't. Until, when you start to join the dots, it most certainly is.

The approach is very televisual, but it's not always obvious where the connective tissue is, and the reason for some of the dramatic choices is often not clear. It makes it hard, in particular, to develop a feel for many of the (many) characters, or see how they slot into the overall narrative. But when you come across the *aha!* moments when you realise that a character in one part of the sprawling timeline connects, appears or echoes in another part of the story you smile, and persevere for more.

Some scenarios and timelines work better than others. The Bobby/Jones/Gracie timeline (early 60s, Pasadena and Tuscon) anchors the rest of the narrative and although it's not without its head scratching moments, it's engaging and inventive. The Keisha (1990s scriptwriter) timeline is interesting and well presented too, as are the multiple deaths in space subsections. If none of this makes any sense at first, welcome to the club. 'The more the Perceived World around them didn't make sense the more they went – yeah - *loco*.' Jones says, in the middle of an existential conversation while having his feet massaged. Indeed.

It feels like you're watching a bank of TV screens all tuned to different channels with the sound dialled high on each one, making it impossible to concentrate on the football. Fans of chaos and complexity will enjoy it. Me? I'll take the blue pill.

(Mark Bilsborough)